Your Husband, My Man
Part One
By: K.C

D1515920

Your Husband My Man
-A Novel Written by-
KC Blaze

Copyright © 2014 by True Glory Publications LLC
Published by True Glory Publications

www.urbanfictionnews.com

platinumfiction@yahoo.com

Twitter: @26kessa

Cover Design: Michael Horne
Editor: Grammarly

Acknowledgments

I would like to take a moment to thank God for blessing me with a gift. The gift to tell a story is something I value greatly and don't take lightly. I would like to thank my family, thank you for your patience with my long hours on the computer. Thank you for listening to my ideas and sounding shocked at all the right moments. I would also like to thank anyone who take a moment to read this story. Thank you for giving me a small amount of your time, for allowing me to introduce you to my characters. Thank you for walking with them through all of the ups and downs of their crazy life choices. I hope you enjoy the first in this series!!!

Before You Judge
Lauren

The engine to my late model Jaguar purred like my pussy when Tori came around. Life is funny, I was parked a few houses down from my best friend Misha's house waiting on her husband, but my man Tori to come outside. A few minutes after my text, I saw him walking toward the car from my rearview mirror. His sexy caramel face had a hint of irritation but I didn't care because I had needs too.

"Lauren? I told you not to come to the house when she's home. I don't need my neighbors talking shit." I sped off before he could finish his sentence.

"You're mad now but you'll be happy in just a few minutes." I glanced his way, his eyes softened.

"Oh yeah, why's that?" Tori looked my way. I grabbed his strong hand and placed it in my lap. His fingers moved my black mini skirt up my thigh and landed at my freshly shaven pussy.

I couldn't park fast enough. I no longer felt guilty about screwing Misha's man simply because she deserved it.

She practically forced Tori to propose, constantly nagging about getting married and having a husband just to get him and not treat him right. I was the last of my friends to be single but for a very good reason. Being the mistress was much more lucrative. I only date married men with long pockets because they have limited time and too much to lose. Arnold Blake is my main sugar daddy, a partner at one of the top law firms in Atlanta and a very married man. Tori is my boy toy and I prefer to keep it that way, for now.

I pulled over at one of our frequent quickie spots. A dark area concealed by bushes, tall hedges, and shadows deep enough in the local park to not be seen. I shimmied my skirt up over my round ass before sitting on his lap. Tori loved every inch of my 5'8 frame. Thick hips, well-sculpted calf muscles, small waist, and full 38D cups were covered in milk chocolate skin. He put his head back on the leather headrest. The hardness of his ten inch dick pressing into my wetness.

"You still mad?" I asked between kisses to his neck, cheeks and lips. He shook his head no, using his hands to squeeze my tight ass. I knew he wouldn't be, especially knowing he had Misha's out of shape ass to go home to. She wasn't a big chick but she didn't keep it tight either, things sagged and she stopped getting her hair and nails done soon after the honeymoon.

I rubbed his biceps, which always had a way of making me wet. His body was insanely muscular while other dudes stopped at a six pack he stomach crunched his way into an eight.

"I want that dick now." I panted in his ear, my hips gyrating on his hardness. I needed him to unzip his jeans, like yesterday.

"Oh, you want this dick?" He loved hearing me talk dirty so that's what I gave him.

"Yes, give it to me Tori," I was practically bouncing on it now. He unzipped his jeans, unleashing the beast and before he could say anything I slammed down hard enough to feel his dick in my uterus. We haven't had sex in over a week because Misha has been tightening his leash. Tori impatiently pulled my shirt and bra down, my dark nipples now in his face. He took his time working his tongue on one while I did my magic on his rod. Arnold's old ass never made me feel like this but he had things Tori didn't, so they balanced one another out.

The car windows were fogging quickly, within minutes the car was rocking back and forth. I didn't care about anything or anyone but the two of us in that exact moment. It wasn't until after he gripped my waist and pressed me down hard on his dick that I knew he was about to cum. I loved seeing the look of satisfaction I gave him right before he blew his load. He growled low and sexy and held me close to him.

"Damn girl. I swear I should have married yo ass." His comment made me laugh. I would never have married him no matter how sexy he was. Marriage changes everything. I eased off of his lap slowly. He reached for the unscented baby wipes from the glove compartment, wiping himself down carefully. I always made sure I never wore perfume so it wouldn't get on his clothes. I didn't even wear lipstick to avoid any slip ups. He zipped up as I headed back in the direction of their house.

"Drop me off at the 7-eleven. I told Mish I was going to the store." He pointed in the direction of the large bright lights a few blocks down. I laughed before pulling up to the brightly lit parking lot.

"Text me tomorrow." He requested before opening the passenger door.

"Wait, did you delete the last message I sent you?" I asked. Men could be stupid and I didn't have time to rock the boat.

"Yeah." He answered too quickly.

"Let me see." I held out my manicured hand for him to show me the phone. He scrolled through his text messages and showed me that he did delete my last message. Leaning forward in the car he kissed me full on the lips.

"Alright boo. See ya later." I pulled off in the direction of my house.

Now before you judge, let me be clear that I love my girl Misha but she is no different than a lot of these chicks out here. They say they want to be married, go all out of their way to snag a dude just so they can start slacking, Tori never complains about what she doesn't do for him but Misha tells me during our daily girl talk. She stopped wanting to go out, she stopped caring about her hair, nails, clothes and she stopped wanting to give it up. Her favorite line is "I didn't marry him to be his hoe." She nags him about everything he doesn't do and never appreciates what he does. She used to work out with me four days a week, kept her hair and nails on point and cooked for him the entire time they were dating. All that went down the drain the minute he put a ring on it.

For the record I didn't go after Tori first it literally just happened. I only date men with both big money and wives and though Tori has a good job as a software developer, he's too new in the company to be pulling six or seven figures yet. That would mean he only met one of my must haves. The day *it* happened I was at my nightclub Seduction when he walked in looking all happy. He asked where Misha was, I told him she changed her mind about coming out. He put his head down, shaking it slowly. I asked what was wrong and he said he wanted to tell her that he got the job. I couldn't believe she wouldn't show up when her man told her that he wanted to come out to celebrate. So I closed off my VIP section, delivered bottles of Moet to his table and only let the hottest people into the roped off section to celebrate.

We partied until two in the morning and he helped me close up the club. When there was nothing left to do we both said good night, standing only inches away from one another and like moths to a flame we started kissing. I used to think people who said that 'it just happened' were a bunch of liars but I swear that is exactly how it happened. Immediately after our wild sexcapade, we felt guilty but found fifty reasons to be alone on several occasions since.

I rode home to take a shower, I needed to get ready for tonight. Arnold was bringing a few of his investor friends to assess the value of my club. I had big ideas and he funded most of them. His wife was never the wiser, which was fine by me. My three story condo was in a gated community in the heart of Atlanta. I entered my pin number into the keypad before driving to my designated parking space. The night air was cool against my sticky skin. I loved making love and Tori was the best to ever do it. I would never tell him that, though.

My cell pinged indicating I got a new message. It was Misha's number

Wyd?

I sent a quick jumping in the shower message so she would know I was busy. It didn't stop her, though.

You going in tonight?

She wanted to know if I was going to be at my club, which was a dumb question cause it was Friday night. Friday's are money making nights so of course I was going to watch my investment. I sent over the message of course, why what's up?

I feel like getting my party on

My response was sarcastic. She always said she was going out but never made it past her front door. 'Yeah right girl, you always talking smack, does Tori know you leaving out?'

His ass in here getting ready for
bed.

But he know, though.

Her response made me smile. I put my boo to sleep. I answered by telling her to be there before eleven if she didn't want to pay at the door. I wasn't holding my breath if she came, cool if not I already knew what was up.

My shower was quick, I wanted to be at the club before Arnold and his friends. I needed to hear everything they were saying. Club Seduction was my baby. I worked my magic on Arnold, within six months he was putting the money down on the building. I had a different sugar daddy at the time and between the two of them I had enough funds to open up the hottest club in town for two years running.

My club wasn't ratchet either and only the hottest chicks and finest dudes could enter. Pretty people produced more pretty people. A few of the hottest music groups came through from time to time which added to the club's hype. I knew how to manage business from my namesake Loren Michaels, my father. He started in the streets but went legit with the money he made. My dad left my mom and took me with him when he found out she was cheating on him with the neighborhood slacker. He always told me if you're going to creep, creep upwards but never hustle backward. I was five when they split up, it's been twenty-two years and I've only seen her once since then. She was cracked out with remnants of pretty still marked across her aging face. But time and life had eventually caught up with her.

I could have asked my dad to front me the money for the club but he liked to teach me lessons around anything he ever gave me. He built his empire in real estate investments owning rental properties in over ten states. I wasn't spoiled like a lot of the bitches running around here with Prada & Gucci but learned to work for everything I got even if it meant being the best mistress money could buy. I was on top of my hustle. If the man I had my eye on didn't get a home cooked meal, I became a chef. If he needed to feel like a man, I became a damsel in distress. I was his living, breathing, walking and talking fantasy. I molded my actions to fit his needs. His dreams were dipped in my twisted reality. I wasn't a gold digger because I wanted more than just money, I wanted power and there is nothing more powerful than a woman who controls a powerful man.

After my shower, I towel dried, moisturized with my favorite scented lotion and stood naked in front of the closet. I needed something that spoke money, professionalism and sex goddess. My eyes landed on a $700 form-fitting lace and metallic beaded Mac Duggal dress gifted to me by an old flame. I've never had an occasion to wear it but tonight was just as good as any. Nothing speaks money like Jimmy Choo heels and I had plenty. The only shoes hot enough to compliment the sparkly dress was my sparkly 4-inch champagne glitter Jimmy Choo sandals. I would pull out all the stops tonight because I needed his friends to invest if I wanted to expand my business and make it grow.

The clock on my nightstand read nine, which meant I only had an hour to get my hair and makeup right before the line at the club started wrapping around the block. Sexy ladies were allowed to enter for free before eleven, which is one of the oldest tricks in the book. Pretty women are used as bait to catch the big money spenders. The more sexy women in your club the more men was willing to spend.

Club Seduction was known for having the best-looking women in the city, which meant it was the first choice for fun. I also made my liquor prices lower than my competition. The cheaper your alcohol the more drinks people buy, the more money I make.

I checked myself in the floor to ceiling mirror by the front door and blew myself a kiss. If I were a man I'd date me. With one click of a button, my Jag was on and purring. I stepped inside turned on my favorite John Legend CD and sped off toward my night club. If this deal went the way I anticipated I would be the number one spot for nightlife in Atlanta. I parked around back but could still hear the thunderous chatter of the party seekers standing in line around the front of the club. Seduction could easily hold two thousand people but I usually only let around fifteen to seventeen hundred in. There were two levels, with only nine to ten bouncers working at all times, six bartenders, and a host of club promoters. Though my club was only open four days a week it managed to rake in a little over fifty thousand a week.

Chris, my dark chocolate, if he wasn't working for me he could get it bouncer was standing by the back door.

"Hey, sexy lady." His deep voice filled the small space between us.

"Hey, things going ok around front?" I asked casually.

"The crowd started about an hour ago." He took my car keys and locked the doors. Chris managed my bouncers and I trusted him with most of the business in the club. He was on his game when it came to keeping my money right, suggesting I install cameras in the bartending areas to make sure nobody tried to cheat me. I did it but like my father always said if you keep your employees happy they will remain loyal.

"Any call outs?" I asked over my shoulder, my heels clicking against the hardwood floor in my office.

"No, everybody's here. Come on Lauren, you know nobody call out on Friday and Saturday nights." We shared a laugh.

"True." I sat down behind my desk. I wanted to have a few of my profit figures ready for Arnold and his guest.

"I'll be back." Chris left my office to make his rounds. I paid him handsomely for two reasons. The first is because I stole him from a competitor and second because he proved himself worthy when we first started. He caught one of the bartenders trying to water down drinks and pocket the extra money and bribe him to keep it on the low. He turned them in faster than I could say you're fired. I was impressed with his honesty and decided he could hang with me for as long as he wanted.

A knock on my door interrupted my search.

"Come in." I yelled through the music. A second later Misha's head popped into the office.

"What! You finally came out." I yelled excitedly. Surprised she actually made it.

"I was tired of being in the house all damn day girl. Ooh look at you, who you trying to impress?" she asked with her hand on her hip.

"Arnold is coming tonight with a few investors. I'm trying to upgrade Seduction's status."

"Why you ain't tell me? I would have threw it on." She asked with a semi-stank face. I gave her the once over, she wore a pair of black satin skinny leg pants that complimented the curve of her backside. A white drop neck shirt that revealed enough cleavage to turn heads and her hair was pulled into an upside down French braid in the back and cascading curls up top.

"You look hot so stop tripping. So why you ain't ask Tori to come with you?" I had to act normal or she would catch on.

"Cause, you don't bring sand to the beach. Now come on I ain't wasting my night back here." She danced her way out of my office leaving me to finish looking for paperwork.

Party Favors

Lauren

Once I located the club's profit sheets I placed them in a folder in the top drawer to my desk before locking it. Now, I could enjoy my night while waiting for Arnold to get here. I knew he planned on waiting til about midnight to show up, which would allow the club time to fill up. I walked over to the bar for a sex on the beach and spotted Misha dancing with a brown skin cutie.

"What'll it be?" Dom, one of the hottest bartenders here asked.

"Give me a sex on the beach." I leaned in so he could hear me over the dance music. A tall light skinned brother with curly hair rocking a nicely fitted gray Valentino Italian suit without the jacket turned to face me.

"Interesting choice." He looked over at Dom with a twenty in his hand before reordering my drink.

"Give her the French Cosmo." Dom looked at me waiting for my decision. Sexy suit didn't know who I was so I decided to play along. I nodded my head yes to Dom and he began to make my drink.

"Do you have a habit of choosing ladies drinks?" I asked with my back leaning against the bar and both elbows resting on the counter.

"Only when I know the owner." He stated.

I raised an eyebrow. I was sure I didn't know him so this must have been his pick up line. I fiend interest.

"You know the owner?" A smile played on my lips. Dom now shaking his head in disbelief.

"Yes, he's a friend of mine." The handsome liar continued his fabrication. I laughed when Dom placed the drink in front of me.

"Here you go, *boss*." Dom put emphasis on the word boss, causing pretty boy to back up, now a few shades of red.

"I'm a she, not a he, but if I am ever in the market for a liar I'll be sure to look you up." I took my drink and walked over to Misha.

"Girl, you better relax before you sweat out all your curls," I whispered into her ear. She only smiled and continued to dance with her designated boo for this song.

"What you drinking?" she asked. I gave her my glass to take a sip.

"This is good, what is it?" she asked while holding the glass up to the light like she could identify its ingredients just by looking at it.

"A French Cosmo. The guy over there ordered me one." I nodded my head in the direction of the bar. She looked over my shoulder.

"Who pretty boy?" She laughed.

"Yes, him. Hold on I see Arnold, I'll be back." I left my drink with her as I walked through the crowd. A few sexy club goers stroked my arm as I passed. My sugar daddy's eyes lit up when he saw me. He leaned in and gave me a kiss on the cheek. Two tall, dark and handsome men stood a few feet behind him.

"Hello honey, you look gorgeous as always. I want you to meet a few friends of mine." Arnold stepped aside to allow me to shake each of his guest's hands.

"Lauren, I'd like you to meet Charles Johnson and Keith Walters. Gentlemen this is Lauren Michaels owner of Seduction."

"Nice to meet you," we all said in unison.

"Let's go to my office, it's a bit quieter." I turned to lead the way with each man staring at my voluptuous assets. When we reached my office I used the walkie talkie on my desk to tell Chris to be on alert. Once everyone was seated I closed the door behind us and walked seductively around to my desk.

"I'd like to start by thanking you for your time." I began the conversation. Arnold gave me a nod of approval.

"Now, what we're looking for is not just an investor but a business-minded partner. Someone who knows the entertainment business." Arnold started his undoubtedly planned speech. I sat back and let him do most of the talking. I was sure that once he planted his seeds they would see its potential with the tour.

The club met all of the city's zoning requirements, I had my liquor license and we were already turning a profit. I made sure I had plenty of great reviews on major review sites and my dad gave me his website designer to make sure we had a hot and interactive website for anyone looking to see how we partied. The investors would only be giving me cash to do major marketing and promotion as well as fund a few more of my ideas. On cue, I unlocked my drawer and gave Arnold the profit reports I had ready. Both men looked impressed, nodding in agreement with

Arnold's grand statements. I had to admit he was a pretty smooth talker, that's probably why he chose the legal profession.

"So, Ms. Michaels how are you planning to spend the money?" Keith looked my way, eyes oozing with interest. I turned on my sexual magnetism.

"I have a few ideas for commercials that will extend the club's reach. My research has already shown the cost versus the return of investment. As you can see on the report, club Seduction is already making over fifty thousand dollars a week. Those figures are based on four days. With my ideas, we can open six days a week to maximize income potential." I stood up and walked to the front of the wooden table. All eyes followed the sway of my hips until I sat on my desk and crossed my legs. I knew then that the deal was sealed but I continued throwing numbers around until I had a verbal go ahead.

"How about we give them a tour Lauren?" Arnold stood first and adjusted his pants. He gave me a quick wink no one else picked up on. Charles, Mr. Sexy personified extended his hand to help me from my desk. It annoyed Arnold but he remained cool. I sashayed out of the office, giving a grand tour of the building. There was plenty of eye candy to go around. The half-naked ladies gyrating in time to the music was more than enough to convince both men to sign on the dotted line. The one thing I knew well was men thought more with their lower half, which meant their Johnson's and their wallets. Club Seduction was a pure money maker so they would have plenty of money and lots of ass to choose from.

After the tour I walked them out front, shaking their hands again.

"It was nice meeting you Lauren, I would love to go out for a drink later." Charles boldly chimed in. His request was intercepted by Arnold.

"I'm sure a woman as beautiful as her has a very jealous man at home." I heard his jealous tone but wasn't sure if his friends picked up on it, I laughed unintentionally.

"He's right, thank you for the offer, though, you're kind." I politely declined the offer. No need biting the hand that made the deal, besides I would see Charles again alone I was sure of it. Arnold did the 'I will call you later' hand signal. I nodded and walked back into the club to find Misha. I wanted to celebrate with my good news. I was about to take Atlanta by storm. I couldn't spot her for a few minutes until I saw a mess of curls sitting by the bar. She was nursing a drink and flirting with Dom. Flirting was a part of his job, I even allowed them to give one pretty girl a free drink but only if it meant he said it was coming from a big money spender. You pick up women on your own dime was my philosophy.

"Girl, guess what?" I asked excitedly.

"What?"

"I closed a big deal tonight. I'm about to be the hottest thing in Atlanta." I practically sang the words out of my mouth. She gave me a sideways glance before fixing her face into a smile. I was too happy to care. I dragged her out to the dance floor and partied like it was my birthday.

"We should do something to celebrate. Let's double date. You can bring Arnold." She leaned in and shouted in my ear. My heart nearly dropped to the floor. I pretended not to hear her but she repeated herself louder.

"Ok, I'll let you know." I continued to dance to the music, but my heart was pounding behind my chest. I wasn't worried about being in the same room with Tori and Misha but I've never brought Arnold around Tori before and I didn't want Tori to catch feelings. It would be awkward for sure. Tori was the first dude I was with for fun and not because I had an ulterior motive.

"We can do lunch tomorrow." She wouldn't give it up.

"Ok, I'll check with Arnold ok?" I wanted to squash the conversation. I would need to get her real drunk to make her forget she ever asked.

Nothing is what it Seems
Tori

Misha came in the house kicking her shoes across the room. Slamming the front door loudly then tiptoed in the bedroom like she didn't want to make me wake up. I rolled over in bed to look at her with an 'are you serious?' face.

"Why you woke?" she asked in the same moment she dropped on the mattress.

"You woke me up is why I'm woke. You drove home drunk?" The alcohol was coming from her pores.

"No, Lauren drove me." Her words were slurred. Just the mention of Lauren's name made me wish she were here.

"Damn, how much did you drink? You smell like a distillery." I had to turn my face away from her. I expected her to get a little wasted but I didn't expect to see her pissy drunk.

"You don't have to be rude about it." She snatched my pillow from under my head.

"Help me take my shoes off," Misha demanded in an almost incoherent voice.

"You've got to be kidding me. Are you serious?" I yanked the covers back and got out of the bed. It was four o'clock in the morning.

"You don't have on any shoes, Misha. Get up, come on." I grabbed her by the arm and pulled her out of bed.

"Where we going? Why you yelling?" She stumbled around even with me holding her up. I walked her to the bathroom, set her on the toilet and turned the tub faucet on. If I had to sleep next to her I was going to clean her up first.

"Take off your shirt," I instructed her with one hand under the water to test the temperature.

"You do it." She lifted her shirt slightly over her belly button like she wanted to seduce me.

"Misha come on, stop playing."

"I'm not playing motherfucka, you my husband right? You can undress me." She shouted close to my face with her alcohol-infused breath. I inhaled deeply before slowly removing her shirt, then I unlatched her satin pants and tried to slide them under her butt. She didn't lift up so I had to rest her arms on my shoulders and pull her up by her waist to get them off completely. I removed her panties last and watched my wife sit naked on the toilet before I turned to add her favorite milk and honey bubble bath to the water.

"Come on, step into the tub." I grabbed her arm again to lift her.

She stepped in without a fight but she didn't sit down.

"Get in with me." She slumped her shoulders like a helpless doll baby.

"It's four in the morning." I looked for an excuse.

"Tori, we used to take baths together. Please get in with me." She was right, we took baths together all the time. I pulled down my blue basketball shorts and boxers before stepping in the tub behind Misha. I sat down first and she sat down after, leaning her back into my chest. The water was still running so I had to push us forward to turn it off. We sat in silence for a few minutes, bubbles foaming up around us. I felt her body tremble before I heard her soft cries. I didn't know if she was crying because she was drunk or because she was thinking about something so I just wrapped my arms around her and held her tight.

I wasn't sure when things got bad between us, she changed after we got married. I expected it, though. All of my homies said their girls flipped the script before the ink was dry on the marriage certificate. I just didn't know how much she'd change.

"Why you crying?" I whispered into her hair.

"Lauren just got a deal to make her club blow up and I don't have nothing." I felt a bit conflicted I was happy for Lauren, she was really doing the damn thing but Misha was my wife and I hated seeing her cry.

"Look, you have me. No matter what any other broad is doing you still better than all of them." I spoke into her hair.

"Really?" she kissed me on my chin and neck.

"Hell yeah, you're smart as hell Mish and you can do whatever you want if you stop walking around depressed all damn day." I grabbed her pink loofah, dipped it in the water covering it with bubbles and started washing her back.

"Oh, before I forget, we going on a double date tomorrow." Her head dropped to her chest.

"With who?" I asked.

"Lauren and Arnold." Her words were still slurred. I stopped rubbing her back for a brief second. My jaw tightened involuntarily.

"She still seeing old boy?" I asked nonchalantly. I wasn't supposed to care, cause after all Lauren was just my jump off. I tried to tell myself that but it wasn't working. I didn't feel like being in the tub no more and quickly washed Misha and helped her step out and back into the bedroom. I gave her two Motrin from the bottle in the medicine cabinet above the faucet, she drank them down with the water from the sink.

"Can you hold me?" She asked once we was up to our chins in blankets. I wrapped one arm around her until she fell asleep. I wished it were that easy for me to doze off, but knowing I would have to sit at a table with Lauren and a dude she was seeing kept me awake. I knew how to play it cool, though.

We both slept through the alarm clock, not getting up until eleven fifteen.

"What time is it?" Misha asked with her eyes closed. I took a quick glance at the clock on the nightstand.

"Almost twelve."

"Damn babe, we about to be late for lunch with Lauren. Come on." She yanked the blankets off of me and nudged me to get up with her feet. The only thing that flashed through my head was how fly I would need to look when we went out. Though Lauren would be there with old boy I was going to make sure she wished she was there with me.

There was something about Lauren that made me want to risk it all. She was there for me even when my wife wasn't. I know it's wrong to commit adultery but when people be quoting those bible scriptures I don't hear them saying anything about it being ok for a wife to talk down to her husband or make him feel like he don't have feelings just cause he's a man. I lost count of how many times Misha told me to shut up or that my opinion was stupid. I wouldn't have enough time to go over the amount of names she's called me or the threats to have her brothers come kick my ass, simply because I disagreed with her point of view.

I could honestly say she wasn't the same woman I asked to marry and if I could do it all over again I would think about it long and hard before moving forward. I couldn't look Misha in the eye for an entire week after my first time with Lauren. Eventually, the little things Lauren did for me made me feel good. She sends me sexy text messages calling me gorgeous. She asks me how my day went and even cooks for me a few nights a week. I get everything I need from my wife from her but it's getting harder not to catch feelings.

While Mish was confirming things with Lauren through text messages I stood in my closet looking for something to show off my biceps. Lauren loves my arms, shoulders and chest, which I put a lot of energy into sculpting.

"We're eating at the Optimist, Arnold's uppity ass picked it," Misha called over her shoulder. I heard about the seafood joint a while back and couldn't wait to go. My clothes were on point with a short sleeve light blue and purple plaid Frangelico button down, unbuttoned over a black tight fitting black t-shirt, dark denim jeans and my black leather Prada shoes. I lotioned up, splashed on a small amount of my expensive ass Himalayan Creed cologne, I bought it right after I got the job as a gift to myself.

"You ready?" I asked Misha but I knew she wasn't, she always took a million years but especially when it involved one of her girlfriends.

"Don't start rushing me, please. I just gotta curl my hair and I'm done." She snapped from the bathroom. I chose my battles carefully and decided it would be better to just wait on the couch.

"Well, I'm downstairs," I spoke through the bathroom door and headed down the steps

Thirty minutes later and she was finally ready to leave the house. If I didn't know how long it took Lauren to get ready I would be mad for making me wait. We jumped into our silver Dodge Challenger with me behind the wheel. It had a hint of alcohol still in the air from last night.

"Do my makeup look right?" she asked turning from the mirror in the sun visor.

"I'm driving babe, I can't see it. I'll tell you when we get there." I answered without looking her way.

"Ok." Misha flipped the sun visor closed and made herself comfortable.

"Don't forget to talk to Arnold, I don't want him feeling left out and please try not to say anything embarrassing when we get there. You know how you do." She rolled her eyes while giving me the lecture.

I ignored most of it, I couldn't stop thinking about seeing Lauren in hopefully something sexy. I was already planning on banging Misha's back out tonight, cause I was always turned on after seeing Lauren. We pulled up to the Optimist and I did a quick sweep with my eyes to see if

Lauren's Jaguar was parked anywhere but it wasn't. Like a gentlemen I walked around the car, held my wife's door open and we walked arm and arm into the restaurant. Here Misha was giving me a lecture on not being out of line but she walked in wide-eyed like a ghetto chick who ain't never been nowhere. For a moment, I hoped Arnold canceled so it could be just the three of us but no such luck. I could see Lauren's gorgeous brown face surrounded by loose curls sitting at a table by the window. Her face lit up when she saw us getting closer.

Stand up, stand up, please stand up. I thought to myself so I could get a good look. She read my mind and stood up from the table to hug Misha. I let my eyes quickly scan her short, tight and sexy black skirt a silver beaded tank top shirt with a black form-fitting blazer.

I extended my right hand to Arnold's left, though I didn't want to. I could tell he was a professional from his three-piece suit.

"Tori" I introduced myself before Lauren took over.

"Arnold you remember Misha? This is her husband Tori, Tori this is Arnold." She looked down when she said his name. I already knew his name but wanted to know who he was to her.

"Hey, nice to meet you brother," Arnold said while taking my hand. I hated this dude already. I pulled out Misha's chair before we both sat down.

I looked intently on Arnold's face for a second longer than I should. He put his arm around the back of Lauren's chair.

"So, Tori what type of work do you do?" he threw out the question casually but I knew he was sizing me up.

"I'm a software developer over at Jackson and Kline." I adjusted myself in my seat.

"Wow, that's interesting. What type of software." He continued to prod.

"Its top secret until after it's presented to the market. How about you? What do you do?" I briefly glanced at Lauren who was staring at me hardcore.

"I'm a lawyer, well partner of Rosen, Marshal, and Blake law firm." I wanted to smack that cocky smirk off of his face.

"I didn't come here to talk about work and I'm thirsty. Do they have waiters?" Misha interrupted and started looking around the large room.

"Yeah, they do," Lauren stated casually.

Throughout lunch, Lauren avoided eye contact, which was driving me mad and Arnold stroked her arm too much for my taste. Close to the end of dinner she excused herself to go to the bathroom, I waited a few minutes before I stood up and headed in that direction. I stood outside of the ladies room until she came out.

"Are you serious about that dude?" I asked as soon as I saw her.

"Tori, what are you doing?" she asked.

"You heard my question, that dude is an arrogant son of a bitch." I didn't want to be as irritated as I was but I couldn't help it.

"You're here with Misha and I'm not mad." She moved in for a kiss. I dipped my head low enough to give her one.

"That's different." That was the only answer I could give.

"It's cute that you're jealous sexy but Arnold is helping me fund my ideas for Seduction."

"I still don't like him." I pressed her against the wall and gave her one hell of a kiss. We heard footsteps behind us and she quickly tapped my chest and walked back toward our table. It was a short white women headed toward the bathroom. I darted into the men's room just missing Misha by a few seconds.

I used the bathroom and took my time washing my hands before going back out. I would have to pretend to be cool with this dude. Both Misha and I walked out of the bathrooms at the same time.

"Babe, is it me or is Arnold a piece of work?" Misha asked me first. So it wasn't just me.

"It's not just you if he say one more thing about his firm I'm going to pimp slap him," I answered, making her laugh.

"I'm ready to leave so." Misha smoothed her skirt while we walked back over to our section. The waiter put the check in the center of the table. Arnold reached for it first.

"No, its ok dude I got it," I said before he could grab it.

"It's quite alright my brother I can pay it this time." Arnold picked up the bill looked it over and took out a credit card to pay. I waited for the waiter to walk away before reaching in my pocket to leave a tip. I placed thirty dollars on the table making both ladies whip their necks in my direction. I stood up first, smoothed my pants and pulled Misha's chair back.

"It was nice meeting you Arnold, Lauren be safe. Come on babe." I instructed Misha to hurry up.

"I'll call you later," Misha told Lauren as we both walked out of the restaurant. I didn't want to sit there any longer than necessary.

"You want to go catch a movie?" Misha asked me.

"Sure, but I want some first."

"You want some of what?" She gave me a sideways glance as she asked the question.

"You know" I answered as we both sat in the car.

"Nigga, can I enjoy one day without you coming at me hard for sex?" She elevated her voice and rolled her eyes in my direction.

The Truth Is
Misha

I couldn't believe how bougie Lauren's dude was. I saw how he was trying to challenge my man but he ain't have nothing on Tori, I didn't care if he was the damn president of the United States of America. I didn't feel like having sex with Tori tonight, though, especially since I knew I had other plans later on. We drove in silence to the movie theater, I didn't care. He didn't want to hold my hand on the way into the movie.

I didn't mean to push Tori away but I am battling my own demons, things he would kill me over. No one would have known we came together with how far away he stood from me. I knew he was mad because he couldn't get what he wanted. Sex, however, was the last thing on my mind, the movie was just a distraction. I didn't want to be home alone with him right now.

After the movie, we rode home with me looking out the window and him keeping his eyes straight ahead. It was ok if he stayed angry, for now anyway. I got out first, slamming the car door behind me. I walked in the house before he even hit the lock button on his car keys. My mom said the mail I've been waiting for was at her house. I jogged up the stairs into our room so I could change. My feet hurt from my damn heels but I could finally take them off.

"Is now a good time?" Tori yelled up the steps sarcastically.

"A good time for what?" I answered with an attitude in my voice. I would have to pick a fight but he should be used to it by now.

"Misha you know what the fuck I'm talking about." He was irritated.

"All you ever want to do is fuck Tori, why is it so hard for you to just be here with me without doing nothing?" I yelled while sliding a t-shirt over my head. His voice came through closer now.

"What the fuck are you talking about? You're my wife when the last time you gave me some? Huh? You can't even answer that cause it was too damn long ago." He was standing in the doorway when I turned around.

"That's all we ever do nigga and I'm tired of feeling like that's the only thing you want me for." I knew I was throwing low blows but I wasn't feeling up to sex and I knew he wouldn't understand that. I pushed passed him to get my sneakers from the closet.

"Where you think you going?" he tried to block me from getting my shoes so I pushed him out the way.

"I'm not playing with you boy, move the fuck out of my way now Tori. I'm going to my mom's."

"You ain't going nowhere." He grabbed me by the waist playfully.

"Get off me, Get the hell off of me now." I pushed him hard enough to make him fall onto the bed and grabbed my sneakers. I ran down the stairs, grabbing the car keys and walked outside to the car. I hated being a bitch toward him but I needed to figure out a few things. Hopefully the mail my mom has will answer some of my questions.

I drove off barefoot in the direction of my mom's house. When I got there I parked and put my sneakers on before knocking on the front door. My little brother Jerry opened it after the second knock.

"What you want?" He asked ignorantly.

"Not you ugly." I pushed passed him.

"Where's mommy?" I asked on my way to the kitchen. My mom was sitting there looking tired as usual.

"Hey, baby." She greeted me. I put a quick kiss on her forehead.

"Hey, mom."

"Your mail is on that table over there." She pointed in the direction of her China cabinet. I walked over slowly, my breath caught in my throat.

"I'll be upstairs for a min," I told her before walking to my old room. The letter burned in my hands. I walked into the room I grew up in, that no longer felt like I ever dwelled there. I flopped on my bed and looked down at the envelope.

Life Adoption Center

Misha Carter
1213 Peachtree Rd
Atlanta Ga

It took a minute for me to open the letter. I ripped the top before I could think about it. The black typed letters on the white paper jumped out at me. Julie, an adoption counselor sent me a letter saying it would be ok if I wrote letters to my son, our son. Tears ran down my face like a running faucet. My secret could ruin my marriage and it was all my fault. When Tori and I were eighteen I got pregnant but I never told him, instead I broke up with him starting college was going to break us up anyway. I couldn't bring myself to have an abortion so I went through the pregnancy and placed our baby up for adoption. A year later and a half later I ran into Tori and we got back together but I couldn't find the right words to say. Eventually, we got married, he started talking about having kids so I tried but we've had two miscarriages so far.

Having him touch me makes me see how fucked up I made things. God was punishing me by killing off any chance of us having a baby. If I told Tori he would want a divorce and there would be nothing I could do to stop him. A light knock on the door distracted me for a moment. My mom peeked her head around the door.

"Can I come in?" she asked before walking through the threshold. I wiped away my tears.

"You ok?" she asked.

"Yes, I'm fine." I lied. She saw through me, though.

"I know facing the truth is hard baby, but sometimes we have to let go and let God. You and Tori have been married for a while now, so you have to trust that he'll understand and forgive you." I wanted to believe her but I knew this would be unforgivable.

"But mama, I've been treating him so bad lately. He wants kids but I keep miscarrying." I spoke between tears. My mom wrapped her arms around me and stroked my hair.

"Give it to God Misha, you did the best thing for you at the time. Now you have to live with that decision but baby I'm going to pray to God for you. If God can forgive you, I'll pray that your husband can too." I cried like an oversized baby in my mother's arms. I wasn't going to tell

Tori until I found the right time and who knows when that will be."

I spent a few more hours at my mom's until it started to get dark.

"I'm going to go, mom, he's probably mad at me." I grabbed the letter, putting it in my purse before walking back to my car. I took a deep breath before pulling off. I needed to fix this before it couldn't be fixed.

Close Call
Lauren

Lunch with Tori and Misha was extremely awkward, especially how they left quickly. After me and Arnold left the restaurant he wanted to go back to my house for a quickie but I told him that I had to do a few things, I gave him a memorable kiss with a promise to get with him tomorrow. He wasn't happy with waiting but he knew I would put it on him when he did get it. I really didn't have much to do but I wanted to sit in my condo in nothing but my panties and bra and think about the day's event. I would be heading over to the club around ten so I had a few hours to waste.

My cell phone pinged twice indicating I had two messages, both from Tori. He was upset, he said he and Misha had a stupid fight and she left him at home alone. Despite my better judgment, I told him to meet me at the 7-eleven in thirty minutes. He looked real good earlier, so, of course, I was willing to head over there. Before I reached the lit convenience chain store I spotted him still wearing the same outfit he had on from lunch. I pulled up, unlocking the door so he could jump in.

"You really need to get a second car," I told him right before our lips met. He held me by the back of my head gently, his tongue traced my lips just enough to ignite a flame in my lower region.

"Boo, what's wrong, you know we don't do PDA this close to your house?" I laughed while pulling away. My foot hit the gas and I drove in the direction of our quickie spot.

"No, I want to go to your house." He stated matter of factly.

"Okay," I whispered a bit confused. He never asked to go to my house before and I never invited him. I always thought it would be too much like real if he came over. I figured he must really be upset if he was making this request. I drove back to my house, entered my pin at the gate and parked in my designated parking spot. He got out first, walked around to my door and opened it.

"Damn babe, I see you." He remarked about the house as he took my hand to help me out the car. I led him by hand to my front door. When he walked in he hugged me from behind.

"Did I interrupt something?" he asked, looking at the half full wine glass on the coffee table.

"No, I was having a drink when I got your text," I answered tossing my car keys on my sofa table. I turned around to face him, my arms wrapped around his neck and I pulled him in for a kiss.

"You were real cute at the restaurant," I said between kisses.

"For what? Telling you about your old ass boyfriend." He laughed while kissing me on my neck. His strong hands grabbed me by the hips and lifted me up. I wrapped my legs around his waist as he walked us over to the dining room table.

"He's not my man," I spoke into his neck.

"Oh yeah? Then who is?" I paused. I've never called Tori my man out loud even though we both knew he was. He laid me across the espresso colored table, removed both shirts and hovered over me with his rock hard body. He was waiting for an answer.

"You are." I stared him in the eye and told him that he was mine. I didn't really know what that would mean from now on. He pulled my skirt up before unzipping his jeans. I felt his hardness now pressing into my wetness. I put my hand on the back of his head and moved my hips down into him. My head dropped back in the same moment his ten inches expanded my tight walls.

"That's right baby, I'm your man, tell me I'm your man," Tori instructed me.

"You're my man, damn Tori, you're my man." He felt so good thrusting in and out of my wetness with long, deep strokes. I kissed his biceps, shoulders and his neck again.

"Are you mine?" he asked.

"Yes, I'm yours. Oh, right there." I moved in time to his rhythm. His dick was good as shit. I looked at his gorgeous face, his sweat dripping onto my body. He was working me like he really missed me.

The buzz of my intercom scared us both. I wasn't expected anyone so they must have rung the wrong bell.

"You expecting somebody?" he asked in mid stroke.

"No, they probably got the wrong address." I moved my hips again until the buzzer went off once more.

"Shit. Hold on boo." Tori moved back so I could get up. I walked over to my intercom.

"Who is it?" I talked through the small box.

"It's me, Misha." My heart starting beating out of my chest.

"What the fuck?" Tori whispered nervously while grabbing his shirts from the floor.

"Hold on," I spoke through the box again.

"Where can I go?" He panicked.

"Go in my room?" I rushed him into my first-floor bedroom. I quickly grabbed my robe off the bed and slid out of my skirt. While closing my robe I walked back into the dining room tossing my shirt to the hallway floor. I tried to take a few deep breaths to slow my breathing before buzzing her through the gate. I peeked out of my window to see her lights reflecting back at me.

I opened the door before she could knock. With the fakest smile I could muster I stepped aside to let her in.

"Hey girl, you busy?" she asked looking a bit sad.

"I was just about to take a shower." I lied. I pointed toward the couch for her to take a seat.

"You ok?" I asked though I could only think about her husband laying in my bed.

"Not really, me and Tori had a fight and I went over to my mom's to cool off but he wasn't home when I got back and he ain't answering his phone." She gave me a full run down.

"He probably just need to cool off, he might be with his boys." I offered a reasonable explanation. I watched Misha turn to look around my condo, she inhaled the air making me nervous. I hoped she didn't smell sex in the air or worse. She turned back to face me.

"You're probably right. I need to chill. I keep giving him grief, but I'm tired of him pushing up on me for sex all the time." Her words stung, I didn't know why that bothered me so much. I guess the fact that he was asking her for sex irritated me. I knew she was his wife but if they were fighting about her not giving him any and he called me after, well it made me angry.

"You going to the club later?" she asked but I no longer felt like company.

"Yeah, I better go take my shower." I stood up from the couch indicating it was time for her to leave. She stood up too.

"Alright, I'll hit you up tomorrow then." She said while walking over to the door. I opened it, let her walk through the doorway and locked it behind her. I couldn't get to my room fast enough. Tori was sitting on the edge of my bed fully dressed.

"Good you're dressed," I said sarcastically.

"What's wrong with you?" He asked.

"So, you had a fight about not getting none and you call me like a flunky?" I looked at him incredulously.

"Look, it wasn't even like that. After I saw you at the restaurant I wanted to be with you but obviously that couldn't happen so I mentioned sex to Misha. She said no like usual and we fought about it. I called you because I wanted to be with you anyway." He tried to clear things up.

"Sounds like I was more like the afterthought." I was off my A game but I felt out of control. No man ever had me caring about what he did with his wife.

"Well you weren't." he stood up, unraveling my robe with his fingers pulling at the robe's belt. I backed up but he followed. My robe fell to the floor. He picked me up and laid me across my queen size bed.

"Do I have your permission to show you what I think about you?" he whispered into my ear. I only nodded my head yes, no longer worrying about his problems with Misha. He stood up stripping down to his very sexy birthday suit. *Her ass is crazy,* I thought while looking over his body. Not only was he tall, sexy, gorgeous and hung like a horse but romantic too. I let him stroke us into multiple orgasms.

Now nine o'clock, two hours after our love making session I sat up for air. Tori was lying on his back with his eyes closed on the bed.

"You better get home." I kissed his cheek.

"What you about to do?" he asked with pure interest.

"Take my shower, I have to go to the club tonight. It's Saturday." I answered.

"Damn, that means I have to go home. Why can't I go to the club with you? I'll be your personal bodyguard." He planted a kiss on my arm. I laughed at his joke though I knew he was partially serious.

"Because you can't." I stood up from the bed.

"I would be a pretty damn good bodyguard. Nigga step back, niggas I said step the fuck back." He mocked my security.

"You so silly. Seriously though Misha probably worried." I walked naked over to the closet to pick an outfit.

"She needs to be with her mean ass." He sat up from the bed. We usually never talk about his relationship, I didn't want to start either. I got to hear enough about it from her.

"Don't worry, I'll be thinking about your fine ass all night. I can still feel all of this inside of me." I grabbed his now soft manhood. He smiled a broad smile like those simple words made his whole night.

"Good, you really know how to make a brother feel good." He planted a kiss on my forehead then reached for his pants.

"You want me to ride you home?" I asked placing a red, thigh high bandage dress on the bed.

"No, its ok I'll take a cab."

He googled a cab for their number and called asking them to meet him around the corner. Tori kissed me once more wanting to leave before I got into the shower. I walked him to the door and peeked out the window before opening it. I didn't need her to be sitting out there. Call it paranoia or guilt but better safe than sorry.

"Text me tomorrow." He said while standing in the doorway.

"Did you delete your messages to me?" I asked looking over his shoulder.

"Yes, see look." He turned his phone to show me that he deleted his message from earlier.

"Good. Be safe ok?" I rubbed his hand goodnight. I didn't want to risk kissing in the doorway.

I closed the door behind him making sure it was locked.

Tonight was more than crazy it was a close call. I couldn't tell if she suspected anything or not but it made me nervous anyway. I buzzed Tori through the gate before walking to the shower. Though Misha almost ruined it, I felt a bit different after telling Tori that I was his and he was mine. We didn't fuck tonight, he made love to me. He held me differently, it felt like it could be more than just like. I had to admit it felt good, real good but I knew we could start getting sloppy. I wasn't ready for any drama, especially not with things going so well for Club Seduction. I would need to be more careful. My shower didn't wash away the feeling of Tori throbbing in my lower regions, though.

Apologies are No Longer Necessary
Tori

I walked through the door at exactly ten forty-five with

Misha sitting on the couch. She had a plate of unfinished

food on her lap. She stared blankly at the TV screen.

"Hey," I said nonchalantly.

"Hey? Is that all you have to say? Where the fuck were

you?" She looked my way. I couldn't believe this chick.

"Why do you care? You're not the only person who

can leave the house after a fight." I walked up the stairs. I

could hear the plate hitting the coffee table.

"You got jokes do you?" she asked sarcastically

trailing close behind now.

"Misha, I don't feel like this tonight ok?" I tried to

close the bedroom door before she could walk inside of the

room but she pushed it open forcefully.

"You don't feel like what? Huh? Where the fuck were you Tori?" she wasn't going to let it go.

"Let's be clear ok? You're not allowed to question me about shit. If you wanted to know where I was you should have been home when I left." I turned my back to her.

"Oh really? You want to talk shit now? You had me in here worrying about your ass. I told you I was at my mom's house." She screamed at me walking around to face me. I didn't want her getting to close.

"Good for you. I'm getting tired of your mean ass, I know that much." My words hit her like a punch to the stomach. She backed away from me.

"Oh, you're tired now?" The fight left her voice. I felt her drop down on the bed.

"Look, I'm tired and I want to go to bed. You said what you said earlier and that's cool. Thanks for keeping it a hundred." I kicked off my shoes and removed my button down. She didn't say anything. I couldn't tell if she was crying but a part of me didn't care anymore. We didn't act married and it wasn't because I didn't try. Granted I'm doing some real shady shit right now but even before it got this deep I was giving one hundred and ten percent. She was always pushing me away and making me feel like I was less than a man. Maybe it was time for us to stop pretending.

"Tori, listen." She started to explain but I cut her off.

"Misha, I said I'm tired. I don't want to talk about it right now." I sounded more irritated than I really was but it did the trick, she stood up and left the room. I finished undressing and walked to the bathroom in my boxers. I used a rag and washed my face, chest and my now soft lady killer.

Misha wasn't in the room when I came back, which was fine by me. I didn't want to have a long drawn out conversation especially when I had such a great night with Lauren. Tonight was the first time she claimed me and it felt good to have someone say they wanted me. It was more than six years since I've heard it.

When I opened my eyes it was morning. I looked on Misha's side of the bed she was there knocked out. I didn't feel her get in bed last night. I pulled the covers back so I could go to the bathroom. It was light outside, the clock read nine. I didn't go back to the bedroom but ran lightly down the stairs to get breakfast. I poured myself a bowl of cereal and milk. When I sat at the table Misha walked into the kitchen. She stood in the doorway for a minute before talking.

"Good morning."

"Hey," I responded and went back to eating. Today felt different like I didn't have to tolerate her shit. I didn't plan on it either.

"Can we talk now?" she asked softly.

"No, you already said everything you wanted to say. Don't worry I heard you. I will no longer ask you for sex ok? I will be here spending all the time you'd like together and I won't touch you." I responded with indignation.

"That's not what I was saying Tori." She walked to the table.

"Really? Cause that's what I heard. I ask you for sex too much, which is BS but ok. I heard you, loud and very clear." I couldn't help but be irritated. It's not like I purposely went out looking to step outside of my marriage. Many would say I have no excuse but I say live in my shoes, live with a person who push you away for years then cast your stone.

"I'm sorry ok?" she wanted to start apologizing but I didn't want to hear it.

"Its fine, apologies are no longer necessary." I put a spoonful of cereal in my mouth and stared at the box. I saw the words but couldn't focus enough to actually read them.

"What does that mean?" she asked sarcastically. I slammed my hand down on the table.

"It means I want to eat my damn food." She turned and walked out of the kitchen. It wasn't like her to not give me a fight. One thing I could always count on was her coming full force, ready for battle. I felt bad after she walked away. But what was I supposed to do sit back and let her dictate the relationship? Wait around like a puppy waiting for my master to throw me a scrap of attention.

I lost my appetite, the cereal became tasteless with each bite. I stood up and poured the rest of the cereal down the drain. I flipped the garbage disposal on and waited a few seconds before turning it off and walked into the living room. Misha wasn't there. I flopped on the couch, grabbed the remote and hit the power button. Nothing like a game of basketball to help me forget about things. A few minutes later Misha walked down the stairs. She stood at the loveseat for a second before walking over to where I was sitting. With no words she sat beside me on the couch, cuddled up and rested her head on my shoulder. I didn't shake her off, we both just sat in silence watching a college

basketball game. She was confusing as hell, one minute she

was picking a fight, screaming and yelling like a crazy

person and the next she was sitting under me like she

couldn't get enough of me.

Time to Back off
Misha

I didn't know where he was last night but it really
didn't matter, especially with him saying he was tired of
my mean ass. No matter how angry we've been at each
other, neither of us have ever uttered those words,
insinuating we didn't want to be here. I was taking him for
granted, which made him verbalize it last night. I was never
one to back down from a fight but I knew he was at the end
of his rope so I backed off. When he slammed the table I
realized something about myself, I realized that I knew how
to push. I went upstairs to cry after he hit the table. I turned
the bathroom faucet on and cried into the sink. I didn't
want him hearing me. When I was done I came down stairs
and saw him sitting on the couch. He didn't look as mad as
before and like metal to a magnet, I walked over to the
couch to sit with him.

There was lots of things I wanted to say to him but silence was the only thing that made sense. What was there to say to a person who felt close to walking away? A few minutes before the game ended I stood up to make sandwiches. I knew he didn't finish his food when I heard the garbage disposal. I sliced his sandwich in half, poured him a glass of juice and put a pickle on the side of his plate. I made myself the same and carried it into the living room. He looked a little surprised but took his plate and cup from my hands.

"Thanks." He said as I sat down beside him, setting my plate on the coffee table.

"You're welcome." I answered softly. We ate in silence and just as he promised he didn't make any attempt at touching me. It made me panic, I wasn't used to him not showing me some type of affection.

All of this was killing me and knowing that I would need to tell him about my secret made it even more complicated. If Tori was at the end of his rope now this would surely be what pushed him over the edge. When the game finally ended he stood up to put the dishes away. I didn't know what to say or how to say it. I've never been speechless before so this was way too new for me. Before I could find the words to say he went back upstairs to the room. I walked up behind him.

"I need to say something." I started off.

"Misha please." He stopped me. I was floored, stuck between winning and losing.

"It won't be much." He turned to face me, the words built up in the back of my throat but refused to come out.

"I know I haven't been acting right lately." I continued.

"You can say that again." He mumbled sarcastically. I took that one on the chin.

"It's just that everytime we have sex it reminds me of the miscarriages. It reminds me of what I can't give you."

Tears welled in my eyes. My words were only partial

truths. His shoulders slumped letting me know that my

words hit home.

"Damn." Tori spoke just above a whisper.

"I'm sorry for acting like a bitch, I know you don't

deserve it. I've been walking around here depressed

because I can't stop thinking about it." I continued. I had

him where I wanted him.

He stood up from the bed and walked over to me.

"Misha, I didn't know you were still going through that."

His hands pulled me closer to him. He pulled me in for a

hug. I laid my head on his chest and cried.

"I know, it was selfish of me to keep it from you but I

felt like it was my burden to bear."

"They were my kids too Mish. I wanted them more

than anything. I'm sorry for being such an asshole." He

apologized. I almost felt guilty about making him feel bad

without telling him the whole truth.

"Apologies are not necessary." I gave him back his words. He held me tighter.

"Look, I'm supposed to be your husband right? We're supposed to be able to share these things. I didn't realize you were depressed about the miscarriages. I would have been more patient." I relaxed into his arms. Maybe I could tell him one day without losing him forever. I looked up into my husband's handsome face for a few seconds before lifting on my tip toes to kiss him. His lips didn't move at first but then he began to kiss me back. I loved Tori more than anything and losing him would be devastating. I really did have a good black man so it was time to back off.

I pulled his shirt above his chest and over his head. He took my clothes off quickly and threw me down on the bed. Flesh to flesh, I felt carnal and raw passion for the man I vowed forever too. He must have felt the same thing because he held me very tight. My legs were around his waist as he began to thrust me with hard, strong strokes. He looked into my eyes as he entered me and we both had tears building up. I pressed my fingers into his muscular back, holding on to him for dear life. I wasn't sure what to call what we were doing. He fucked me hard until his body shook from an orgasm. After his convulsions stopped he dropped on top of me crying into the pillow behind my head. I laid beneath him stroking his back and crying into his shoulder.

I wasn't sure how we got to such a dark place but I wanted to fix it, no I needed to fix it.

I promised myself silently to be a better wife to my husband. If we were going to have a fighting chance I would need to become better.

Everything is Right with the World

Lauren

My dad called asking to meet for lunch. I was always happy to see my daddy and not just because he bought me a gift every time either. I showered, lotioned up and sat on my bed to get dressed. I had a new pair of gray skinny jeans I wanted to wear with my black pumps a black tank top shirt and a hot pink off the shoulder belly shirt. He texted me once he was on his way so I locked up the condo and headed out toward the café we were eating at. Today was a good day, I could feel it.

Heads turned when I parked the car and stepped out. My dad was sitting at a round café table on the outside of the restaurant. He waved his hand for me to sit.

"Hi, daddy." I kissed him on the cheek before taking my seat in front of him.

"Hey, baby girl. How are you?" he smiled. My father was a handsome man, three years shy of fifty. He dressed in a pair of jeans, a pink button-down, and a gray blazer. His Cartier watch glimmered in the sunlight.

I ordered you a Pina colada if that's ok. I know how much you love those girly drinks." He gestured for the waitress to come back to the table.

"They're not girly just good." I laughed. My eyes searched the menu for something good to eat. I didn't eat breakfast so I was starving. The young fresh-faced waitress took our order and the menus away from the table.

"So how is everything?" he asked before sipping his Corona.

"Great, I just landed a deal with a few major investors, which means I will be making a few commercials to promote the club." I waited for his response.

"Wow, nice honey. So the club is doing ok then?" he asked curiously.

"Yes, I've been hustling hard to make sure we stay on top of everyone's minds. I hired a social media promotions team a few months ago and they have been creating buzz online. I'm excited." My dad smiled as he watched me talk.

"You know I'm proud of you right?" he asked sincerely. Though I knew he was I couldn't remember the last time he said it. His opinion of me and my success meant a lot to me. The waitress came back with our food and we began to eat.

"I brought you something." He reached into his pocket and pulled out a beautiful blue Tiffany & Co. box. I excitedly reached for it. Opening it with the quickness. I loved jewelry especially when it came from Tiffany's. A beautiful pair of Tiffany Metro 18k white gold and diamond hoop earrings sat on a soft white pillow.

"Awww, daddy I love them," I smiled before replacing my earrings with the ones daddy just bought me.

"Good, now I can tell you my good news." I looked at him curiously. What good news could he have that required $2,700 earrings?

"What news?" I stopped eating to hear this.

"You know I've been dating Shannon right?" I knew the woman he's been seeing for the last two years, but I also knew she was like thirty-five years old.

"Yeah, what about her?" I fixed my gaze on his face.

"I proposed to her last night and she accepted." His smile was spread from ear to ear but my heart stopped beating. Not that I didn't want to see my dad happy but I didn't want it to be with someone who could technically be my sister.

"Dad, she could be my sister." I threw those words at him hoping they took root and he came back to his senses.

He laughed.

"Lauren, I wasn't thinking about babies at twelve years old so no she couldn't have been your sister."

"You know what I'm saying, daddy. I have girlfriends her age." I pouted. I was more upset with having to share my father with someone else. Of course, she was cool now but once they got married she would change him and then I would be forgotten about. I faked a smile.

"Don't worry, we will still be close, nothing will change that." He read my concern. I wasn't convinced, though.

"We are already living together so it's only a matter of legalizing it." He continued.

"Does she make you happy?" I asked him seriously.

"She makes me feel more than happy. I haven't met anyone else like her and though we've been living together for almost a year she hasn't changed things up on me. She loves me almost as much as you do." He winked. I guess I should be happy he found someone he wanted to spend forever with.

"Ok, I guess I'm happy for you but I do have one request." He smiled again.

"Anything." He put his fork to his mouth.

"I want to speak with Shannon before you get married."

"Should I be worried?" he asked with a look of amusement.

"No, I just want to let her know how much I love you and that hurting you is never an option," I answered. He reached across the table and squeezed my hand.

"I love you baby girl and I love that you care about me getting hurt. I will set up a lunch or dinner date for the two of you." I felt better. If Shannon was getting married to make sure her financial future was secure that was fine I could respect it but what she didn't know was that my dad already put me in his will to inherit all of his properties as well as his money. He promised me that he would never change it and even had it drawn up by his lawyer. It was irrevocable so the most she could get was money from an insurance policy. I wasn't worried about her gaining anything but I really wanted to make sure she was in it for my father and not just his wallet.

"We're having an engagement party soon. It's going to be at her sisters. I'll text you her address. Please come ok?" he invited me.

"Will it be in the afternoon? I have to be at the club around ten."

"Yeah, it's at one in the afternoon." He answered with a bit of relief in his voice that I was acting cool about it all.

After lunch, I gave him a big hug, thanked him again for the earrings and walked to my car. That was a lot of information I would need to process. My father was a woman magnet, he was handsome, wealthy and smart so women were attracted to him for as long as I could remember but he never liked anyone enough to propose so I guess I could be supportive. I did like Shannon and she had impeccable taste in clothing.

When I got back to my condo I sent Tori a text message asking if he thought he could get away for a little bit. I tossed my keys and my phone down on the coffee table waiting for his response. Twenty minutes passed and he didn't answer. I tried again, this time, I put three question marks. In the meantime, Arnold called.

"Hey, babe," I answered.

"Hello beautiful, so listen, things are a go on my end. I drew up the paperwork and both Charles and Keith signed on the dotted line. They will be wiring you the funds by the end of today. I hope that makes you happy princess." Arnold sounded excited about his deal-making skills. I had to admit I was impressed with him.

"I am very happy handsome." I flirted.

"How happy?" The hint of curiosity in his voice. I laughed playfully.

"Happy enough to put it on you." I went along with the conversation. I never let Arnold come to my house primarily because I didn't want to bring drama to my house if his wife ever found out.

"Well, I'm only waiting on you."

"Can we meet at the four seasons in two hours? You bring the champagne, I'll bring the wine glasses." I gave him instructions.

"Ok baby, see you in a bit ok?" he blew me a kiss before hanging up. Still no answer from Tori, which made me worry. Usually, he answered within a few minutes. I told myself to stop tripping. Misha was probably sitting close by him. I decided to give Misha a call to tell her the news of my dad's engagement. However, I needed to know what Tori was doing. Her phone rang four times before she answered it.

"Hey, Lauren." She answered.

"Hey girl, what's up?" I asked casually.

"Nothing much. Me and Tori sitting here watching a movie. Why what's going on?" she asked with a small hint of interest.

"I just came back from lunch with my dad. Girl, he proposed to Shannon." I said.

"What?" she perked up a bit.

"Yes, I don't even know what to think about it," I confessed.

"But don't you like Shannon? She's seemed nice when I met her at his cookout last year."

"I like her but it's different knowing she's going to be my step-mom. She's only eight years older than me." I reasoned even though most of my sugar daddies were way older than me and my dad would have a heart attack if he knew I was with anyone older than him.

"If he's happy then you should be happy for him. Lord knows he's been single for way to long as it is." She gave me good advice. I wondered what Tori was doing if he was listening in on our conversation. I wanted to jump through the phone.

"You're right, I just don't want her to be using him or playing games."

"I'm sure your dad is smart enough to smell a gold digger. She has a job though don't she?" Misha asked.

"Yea, she's a magazine editor," I answered. I hadn't thought about it but Misha was right. Shannon has a job that she loves and if she was all about the money she would have probably quit when they moved in together.

"Well, I won't hold you up. Get back to your movie. Tell Tori I said what's up." I started to end the call.

"Lauren said what's up." She told Tori what I said and I waited for his response. I could hear his deep voice speaking in the background.

"He said hey and stop hating on your dad." She laughed. I laughed too and said bye one more time before hanging up. I could breathe, he wasn't ignoring me.

Things Just Got Complicated

Tori

After our talk, I felt closer to Misha. I hadn't realized how much she was hurting about the two miscarriages we had. I thought she was just being mean because she wasn't attracted to me anymore. Now I felt like shit for stepping out on her. I saw the two text messages Lauren sent me but I was with Misha watching a movie so I couldn't answer. I was thinking about slowing things up with Lauren. I couldn't keep cheating knowing my wife was hurting. I liked Lauren way more than I should but right was right. Guilt hit me hard as bricks after making love to Misha. It hit so hard it made me cry during my orgasm. I vowed before God and our families to be the best man I could be to my wife and fucking her best friend didn't add up to that.

When Lauren called Misha I knew she was checking for me. I didn't answer so she wanted to use my wife to find out what I was doing. It made me smile but I quickly brushed those thoughts out the window. When Misha hung up we finished the movie. I was getting hungry so I knew I'd want dinner soon.

"Yo, I'm getting hungry." I rubbed my stomach. Misha looked at me.

"You want me to cook?" she asked

"No, we can go out to eat tonight. You feel like it?" I pulled her closer to me.

"I sure do, where you want to eat?" she asked but I didn't have a clue.

"We can figure it out later." Once the movie ended I hit the power button on the remote. We both stretched and headed up the steps to get dressed. I threw on a pair of jeans and a white t-shirt. I knew Mish was going to take forever to get ready so I put on my sneakers and told her I would wait downstairs.

She surprised me when she came down ten minutes later with a pair of tight jeans, flat sandals, and a blue tank top shirt. Her hair was pulled into a ponytail.

"What?" I said sarcastically.

"What you talking about?" she asked with a smile on her face.

"You, ready in less than an hour it must be about to rain." I played with her.

"Shut up." She laughed while tossing a throw pillow at me.

"Come on babe, I'm hungry." She said while walking to the car. I stood up and started looking for the car keys. I couldn't see them on the coffee table. I walked to the door, she was already sitting in the car. I guess she didn't lock the doors last night.

"Babe. Where the car keys?" I asked.

"I think they're in my purse. It's upstairs, the big black one." She instructed. I closed the door and ran up the steps by twos. I saw her oversized purse sitting on the dresser. I was always told not to look in a woman's purse by my grandmother. Misha gave me permission so I opened the bag and started looking for the keys. She had a makeup case, a small pack of tissues, candy, receipts, I couldn't see the keys so I moved the papers out of my way and spotted an opened envelope. I was about to push it aside to get the keys until I saw the words Life Adoption.

I paused for a second, not really sure why it made me curious. I pulled the envelope from the purse and pulled the letter out. The wind was knocked out of me when I read the words. A woman named Julie was giving Misha permission to write letters to her child. It claimed that Misha was the birth mother to a little boy. What the hell? I asked myself. The weight of the words made my knees weak and I dropped on the edge of the bed. The boy was eight years old. I stopped to think but the information came rushing in all at once.

I heard the front door close but I was frozen. She came up the steps and walked into the bedroom.

"Babe, did you find it?" her words faded when she saw me holding the envelope in my hands.

"Tori, let me explain." She dropped to her knees before me.

"Explain what?" I asked not wanting her to touch me.

"Please, let me explain." She begged.

"Ok, explain to me why this paper is saying you have a son." I crossed my arms waiting for her answer. Tears dropped from her eyes but I was unfazed.

"When we were together at eighteen I got pregnant, I didn't know what to do. I was about to go to college and you were going to another school so I didn't want to tell you. I didn't want you to feel like I was trapping you, so I broke up with you." Her tears were coming in heavy but I remained silent wanting to hear everything.

"I gave the baby up for adoption." My heart dropped. She didn't just say she gave my son away.

"We got back together I wanted to tell you but I couldn't find the words so I figured when we got married we would be able to have more children but I've miscarried and now." She choked on her words.

My head pounded. Here I was thinking she couldn't carry full term and this bitch gave my son away. I couldn't believe what I just heard. I want to hit something. She reached for my hand but I yanked it away.

"Move, Misha move out of my way." I pushed her away from me so I could stand up. I dumped the remaining contents of her purse on the bed, grabbed the keys and walked downstairs.

"Tori? Where are you going?" she screamed after me.

"Don't fucking worry about it." I yelled up the stairs. I couldn't be near her or I would hit her. She just made me feel guilty about screwing Lauren, just to find out that she was playing me this entire time. How do you give away my son and look me in the face for years with a clean conscious? I wanted a kid so bad, especially when we first got married. Misha had me hooked on her ass from the moment I saw her. When I was eighteen, Misha had me wrapped around her pinky finger. I wanted to be spend forever with this chick, she was my first love and when she broke up with me I was devastated. I went to college and couldn't focus, so against my mom's advice, I took a break from school. When I came back a year later I spotted her and we got back together. She motivated me to finish up college. I wasn't about to let her go that easy so I proposed. Had I known that she gave my child away I would have never talked to her.

I pulled out of the parking space with wheels spinning. She was sitting in a heap in the doorway crying. Good, is all I could think. I didn't know where I was going but I was getting there fast. I drove until I parked in front of my mom's house. My nieces and nephews were playing around in the front lawn. I jumped out of the car and walked angrily to the front door. It was open and my mom and sister was sitting in the living room talking. I couldn't speak, I dropped to my knees in front of my mom.

"Oh my God, Tori are you ok?" My sister Tanya asked jumping up from the couch. I cried in my mother's lap. Call me a punk, call me a sucka but I don't care. I was weak and my mother was the only strength I knew strong enough to hold me up.

"What's wrong baby?" My mother stroked my back, her voice filled with worry. I tried to stop crying but I couldn't. All I could think about was my son that I wouldn't get to know and how Misha stole him from me. She didn't give me a say in what happened to him and that he may grow up thinking I didn't want him.

"Tori?" Tanya asked

"Give him a minute." My mom's voice calmed my sister. I could tell Tanya was pacing the floor. I didn't mean to make her worry but I couldn't think about her feelings right now. I took a few deep breaths before I stood up to sit on the couch.

"Now tell me, what's the matter?" My mom asked with wide eyes.

"Me and Misha have been having some problems. She's been distant and not wanting to be intimate so I've stepped out on my marriage. I know I'm wrong and I've made the decision to cut things off." I paused for what I knew was coming.

"Did she find out?" my mother asked with a voice of disappointment.

"No, but I found out today that when she broke up with me back in the day it was because she was pregnant and gave my son up for adoption." The words choked me up. My sister jumped up from the couch again.

"What?" Tanya had fire in the back of her eyes.

"Hold on baby, she did what?" my mother asked in disbelief.

"She gave my damn son up for adoption." I answered.

"How did you find out?" My sister asked.

"We were about to go out to eat and I couldn't find the car keys so she told me to get them out of her purse but I found the letter from the adoption clinic. I'm done." My answer was very certain. I wasn't staying with her, she was crazy if she thought so. My mom wrapped her arms around me again. Misha knew how I felt about having a family. My dad walked out on us when I was six and I refused to be like him. She took my choice away from me with her selfish ass. There was nothing else to say about her and her selfish decisions.

My phone was ringing nonstop but I refused to answer it. I knew it was her calling to explain away the unexplainable.

"Honey, you were wrong for cheating and what Misha did was inexcusable, especially since she didn't come to you with her concerns." My mom's voice cracked and she started crying. I hated seeing my mom cry and it made me hate Misha in that moment.

Hard to Let Go
Misha

My heart nearly jumped out of my chest when I saw Tori holding the adoption letter. I totally forgot I had it in my purse until after I noticed how long he was taking to come back to the car. I ran up the stairs hoping it was nothing but was devastated to find out that he found it. I felt my world crashing down around me and there was nothing I could do to stop it. I should have told him, was the only thing I could think as I dialed and redialed his number. He didn't answer, which made me panic. It could have gone better if I was honest and maybe he could have forgiven me if I would have told him instead of letting him find out on his own.

I didn't know what else to do but call him until he answered. I didn't know where he was, he could have gone to anyone of his friend's houses. He could have gone to his mother's or his sister's house which would be a huge setback. If they knew, there was no getting him back. I never really got along with his sister Tanya, she was a nosy bitch who would crucify me. I dialed his phone again and a woman's voice came through on the line.

"Hello?" His sister Tanya snapped on the other end.

"Tanya, can I speak to Tori?" I knew she wasn't going to give him the phone.

"No, you ratchet piece of work." She was cut off by Tori's deep voice.

"Hang up, I'm not talking to her. She better be gone when I come back too." He spoke loud enough for me to hear. He wanted me to leave.

"Please, Tanya give him the phone," I begged.

"Didn't you hear what he said? He's not talking to you, so get your stuff and leave before I come over there to kick your ass my damn self." She yelled through the phone before hanging up. He had the car so I couldn't drive over to her house. I called the only person I knew who would help me.

"Lauren?" I shouted when she answered the phone.

"Yeah, what's the matter?" she asked sounding concerned.

"I need your help, I'm in some serious trouble and I need you to give me a ride."

"Ok, I'm with Arnold but I'll be there give me like a half hour." She answered. What she didn't know was that a half hour was like eternity.

"Please hurry Lauren, Tori left me. I need to find him." I could tell she dropped the phone.

"Ok, I'll be there." She ended the call and I paced the floor, my mind was filled with fifty things I could have done better. I was young and all I saw was my life ending with a baby. I knew that his dad left him and that he wanted to be a better father to prove to himself that he wasn't like his dad. I knew he would force me to keep the baby. I wished I would have told him now.

When Lauren finally pulled up to the house she looked like I interrupted a booty call. Her hair was a bit messy and her shirt was inside out. I jogged to the passenger side and got in. Soon as I saw her I fell back in my seat, put my face in my hands and cried uncontrollably.

"What happened?" she leaned over and pulled me into a hug.

"I screwed up," I spoke through my tears. "He's not going to forgive me." I continued. Just the thought of that made me cry harder. It took me five minutes to calm myself down. I told Lauren the whole story about the pregnancy and giving the child up for adoption. I told her about Tori's dad not being there for them and how I ruined my marriage by taking his son away from him. She sat in silence for a few minutes speechless.

"When I called his sister answered. I think he's at her house, if not there his mom's." She started her Jaguar and I gave her directions to his sisters. When we pulled up, the lights were out and no cars were in the driveway.

"He must be at his mom's then." She backed out of the block and I led her to his mom's house twenty minutes away. I could see our car parked in front of his mom's house. His sister's red Maxima was parked out front too. I jumped out of the car before she could even park. I didn't have a plan but I was going to throw myself at his mercy and prayed to God he forgave me or at least allowed me to talk to him.

I banged on the front door, no one answered for a few minutes. His sister Tanya swung the door open.

"Oh no, you're not. You're not going to disrespect my mother's house." She yelled on the top of her lungs reaching to remove her earrings. I wasn't in the mood for his sister but I would whip her ass if she stepped in my face.

"Misha get out of here." Tori stepped in back of his sister. I could tell he was crying, his eyes were red.

"No, Tori, please let me talk to you," I begged. A small crowd of neighbors started to gather on their porches.

"I don't have nothing to say to you if you disrespect my mother's house I'm not going to stop Tanya from kicking your ass." He answered. I knew he was angry but letting me and sister fight meant he was beyond pissed. I could feel Lauren behind me. He looked over my shoulder, which made me turn to see her standing there.

"Now, you heard what the fuck he said, so I'm going to give you five seconds to get back into the car and drive the fuck off." Tanya stepped onto the porch. I readied myself for a fight because I wasn't leaving without talking to him.

"I'm not going nowhere." I stood my ground. I just hoped it wouldn't have to come to this. His mother pushed passed both him and Tanya. I didn't expect to cry when I saw her, but the tears started flowing like a damn brook.

"Misha, he doesn't want to talk to you right now. Give him some time to cool down." My mother in law spoke calmly. I could see Tanya back down a little.

"I can't, he's not going to talk to me. I just need to talk to him." I begged with tears in my eyes. I didn't care about looking like a fool in front of everyone crowding around to see some potential action.

Tanya pushed her mom to the side and swung at my face. Her fist landed on my temple. Her mom tripped backward and Tori jumped to catch her from falling. My knees buckled but I came too quickly. I grabbed Tanya by her hair and tried to rip her hair out by the roots. If I couldn't talk to Tori, I was going to take out my anger on his ridiculous ass sister. She swung her fists at my face trying to get me to let her hair go. I pulled her down to her knees by her hair and started punching her in her back. She tried to stand up but I wouldn't let her. I pounded her back repeatedly. She shouldn't have tried me, I showed no mercy. I began kicking her in the thighs.

"Misha stop." Lauren was screaming in the background. I didn't listen. She asked for an ass kicking so I was going to give her one. I only came here to talk.

I loosened my grip on her hair and she sprung back up to her feet. She charged me like a linebacker and we both fell down the four steps to the porch. I could hear people shouting in disbelief. She was on top of me swinging at my face and chest. I reached up to put my hands around her neck, but she kept coming. Tori's hands grabbed his sister, pulling her off me with her still swinging her feet to kick me. Lauren came over to help me up. My mother in law pulled Tanya into the house.

"Get the fuck out of here Misha before I call the cops.
I'm done with you and this marriage." Lauren pulled me
away from the house. I didn't want to let go. I screamed
through tears.

"Tori, please." He walked back into the house and shut
the door behind him. I felt his goodbye with the closing of
the door. I knew there was nothing I could say or do to fix
this.

Lauren drove me back to the house in silence.
"I need to get a few things," I spoke softly. I felt humiliated
in front of her. I couldn't believe things got this bad. I
called my mom to let her know I would need to stay with
her for a little while. I didn't have a job because Tori told
me it was ok if I stayed home while he supported us. I
couldn't believe I let him get away. He really was a good
dude and my dumb ass refused, to be honest with him. I
walked into my home, my wedding pictures laced the
fireplace, pictures of us on our first cruise together. Pictures

of us in Jamaica were all along the walls. I grabbed my wedding picture and my favorite picture of us in Jamaica sitting on the back of a beautiful white horse.

Lauren sat in the car waiting for me to come back out. I took my time walking the stairs. My heart felt empty. I reached for my suitcase out of the closet and filled it with clothes from the drawer and hangers. I grabbed my curling iron and makeup case from the bed. I reached for the letter on the floor and put it on top of my clothes. I zipped my suitcase and grabbed a bag to put my shoes in. I threw in most of my heels and sneakers before dragging everything down to the car. I didn't want to make matters worse by being here when he came back. I would let things cool down before I reached out again.

Eventually, he would have to talk to me, I reasoned with myself. I hated seeing the pain across his mom's face. She looked disappointed with me. Her face ate at my pain. Lauren was texting when I got in the car, but she quickly put her phone down when I opened the back passenger door to put my suitcase in the back. I figured she was texting Arnold.

"To your mom's?" she asked me softly. I only nodded yes before closing my eyes and leaning back into the headrest. We drove in silence, neither of us wanting to speak. When I got to my mom's house my baby brother Jerry was standing on the porch waiting to carry my bags in. He didn't say anything which was helpful.

"I'll call you later," I promised Lauren, not really sure how far away later would actually be. All I could think to do was go in the house, into my old room and cry my eyes out for the loss of my marriage. My mother met me at the door and hugged me. The tears overwhelmed me and I fell into her arms and cried with no end in sight. She just held me with no condemnation, no I told you so even though she told me I should have told Tori back then. She didn't beat me with my decision just held me like a loving mother

holds her broken child.

Double Edged Sword
Lauren

I was in the middle of giving it to Arnold when Misha called. I wasn't going to answer but something told me I should. I reached over to grab my phone, never leaving Arnold's lap. He still held on to my waist moving his hips as I talked. He was angry but understood that my friend had an emergency. My first thought when Misha told me that Tori left her was where did he go? I drove over there with the speed of light. I cared about my friend but my thoughts were with Tori. When she told me what she did, even I was blown away. I knew he was broken up about it while she was in the house gathering her things I was sending him a text me later message. He responded with ok before she got in the car.

I didn't know what to say about the situation. His sister was wrong for swinging first and for a minute Misha was getting the best of her. I felt conflicted about seeing Tori so upset. He looked good as hell, even though he looked furious. I wanted to hold him and make him feel better but I came to support Misha. Things were going to be crazy for a while with Misha calling me every day to vent but she deserved what she got because again dumb chicks always ruin good men.

I couldn't pull off fast enough from Misha's mom's house. I drove a few blocks and parked. Tori's number was programmed into my phone under the word important so I hit his number and listened for it to ring. He answered after the third ring.

"Hey," he spoke into the phone.

"Are you ok?" I asked concerned.

"Not really. Look, I'm still at my mom's I'm leaving in a few minutes so I'll hit you up when I leave ok?" his deep voice was filled with sadness.

"Ok babe, no problem." I didn't want to be a burden especially while he was irked with Misha. I would sit back and wait for him to call. I pressed the end button and drove back to my house. I couldn't believe she would give away his son without at least talking it over with him first.

When I pulled up to my house my phone rang, it was Tori.

"Lauren?" he asked.

"Hey," I answered.

"I need to see you." I couldn't help but smile. I was happy he wanted to be in my company.

"You can come to my house. I just took her to her mom's so she isn't at your house." I informed him.

"Give me your address again." He requested my address so he could write it down. I gave it to him before hanging up. He was on his way. I straightened up the living room and jumped in the shower to wash away any sign of Arnold. I didn't need him lingering on my flesh when Tori came around. After I lotioned up, the intercom buzzed. I walked quickly to the door to press the button.

"Who is it?" I asked.

"It's me." Tori's voice spoke through the box. I hit the gate button to let it open for him, he drove around to my house and parked beside my Jaguar. I was excited to see him but didn't want to seem overzealous especially since he was hurting. He knocked on the door and I let him in.

Tori wrapped his arms around me and I held him in silence for a few minutes.

"Come on sit down, tell me what happened." I pulled him over the couch by the hand.

"Did she tell you what she did?" He asked while sitting. I nodded yes. He started shaking his head.

"Here I was feeling bad last night about her having the miscarriages just to find out that she already had my baby and gave him away." He said. Miscarriages, I never heard about Misha having a miscarriage. I knew she was a bit more depressed than usual but I figured it was about her wanting to go back to school.

"What miscarriages?" I asked confused.

"A few years ago we were trying to have a baby but every time she got pregnant she miscarried around the fourth month. Last night she was telling me how she's been acting mean toward me because of that shit but her grimy ass was keeping the adoption a secret." He practically shouted at me.

"I'm sorry." That was all I could think to say. I laid on his chest, he put his arm around me.

"I'm done with her, seriously I'm filing for a divorce. I can't be with someone who did that to me." I let him continue his rant

"I could forgive cheating, but you gave my child to a bunch of strangers like I didn't matter. How fucking low she must have thought of me to be able to do me like that." He finished. I felt a bit uncomfortable talking about Misha with him. When she did it, I just thought I was getting information on how I could please him or take care of him.

I didn't want to take care of Misha so all of this was irrelevant information. However, I let him vent for an hour before I stood up.

"I'm so sorry that you're hurting honey, she was dead wrong for doing what she did. I'm here though for as long as you need me." I stood over him talking. He put his hands up to my hips, kissed me on the stomach and said thanks.

"Are you hungry?" I asked to change the subject.

"I'm starving." He said.

"Ok, how about we order Chinese and I'll go grab a bottle of Arbor Mist from the fridge." I walked toward the kitchen to go get two glasses and the chilled bottle from the refrigerator. When I came back he had the Chinese food menu in his hands looking over what he wanted. It felt strange knowing I would have him all to myself. I didn't know how to react to that. I usually only messed with married men so it would definitely be new for me.

Time Doesn't Heal all Wounds
Tori

It's been a few weeks since the incident with Misha.
I've spent almost every other day with Lauren. Apart of me
was using her to avoid facing my pain. Misha has tried to
call me a few times since then but I've sent all of her calls
straight to voicemail. I deleted all of her messages before I
listened to them. I canceled her debit cards, so she wouldn't
have access to my money and I even changed the locks to
the house. I wanted no parts of her. I knew I would need to
speak with her soon to serve her with the divorce papers.
The papers came to my job a few days ago but I haven't
gained enough courage to call her to say it's officially over.

My anger subsided but it left hurt and devastation in its
place. It was Friday afternoon, I still had a few hours left in
the office but I was having a hard time concentrating. I
couldn't stop thinking about the son I didn't know existed a
few weeks ago. I wondered what he looked like, what he

liked doing if he had any of my personality traits. Not knowing hurt just as bad as knowing he was somewhere in the world living without me. Lauren sent me a picture message. It was her in a red see through teddy with an 'I bought this just for you' message attached. I couldn't help but smile. She was everything I've been craving since the day I got married. Funny enough, I wanted it from Misha when I said I do.

I took a deep breath, told myself to man up and sent Misha a text telling her to meet me at the house at six o'clock. She didn't respond right away but sent ok a few minutes later. My heart beat hard, making me take a few deep breaths. I wanted to end things civilly but with Misha anything was possible. Lauren had already helped me pack up her stuff last week, so it was sitting in the living room. I knew Misha was shocked if she tried to come by the house when I wasn't there.

I took my time clocking out at the end of my shift. I wasn't in a hurry to end my marriage. My heart weighed heavy behind my ribs. I got in the car and drove toward home. When I pulled up Misha was already there sitting on the porch. I parked and got out slowly. I didn't want to hold any eye contact so I kept my eyes on the front door. After unlocking it I stepped aside for her to enter first. As soon as I closed the door behind me she started talking.

"Thank you for asking me to meet you." She spoke softly but then she froze after seeing her stuff in the living room.

"What's this?" she asked.

"Your things," I answered seriously.

"Tori, I thought you called me over here to talk." Her shoulders slumped.

"Is there really anything to say? I can't think of anything that would make me stay." I answered truthfully. She sat down on the sofa.

"I was wrong ok, I know what I did was foul. I wish I could take it back but I can't." She began to cry. I was unfazed by her tears, which let me know I was really finished with the relationship.

"It goes beyond wrong to me, you stole my fucking son away from me like a thief in the night. You conned me into thinking you were marriage material. I gave my life to you and you spit on it by keeping this from me." I yelled at her. I inhaled pulling air into my lungs until they burned.

"I didn't bring you over here to rehash the past. I want a divorce, I have the papers here for you to sign." I reached in my bag and handed her the divorce papers. My signature was already at the bottom.

"What'? Wait Tori I don't want a divorce." She cried.

"Too bad Misha, my heart ain't in it no more," I told her how I honestly felt.

"Well, I'm not signing the papers. Please give me time to think about it." She begged. My decision was going to remain but I would entertain her request.

"Fine, please take your stuff with you." I walked into the kitchen leaving her there crying on the couch. I could hear her calling a cab. Apart of me wanted to question her but I wasn't sure I'd like to hear the answers, so I let things be. I didn't help her with her luggage when the taxi arrived. She lingered out front for a few more minutes but I stayed in the kitchen ignoring the hell out of her.

People say time heals all wounds but I wasn't sure I would ever get over this betrayal. I wasn't sure I would ever forget it either. My marriage ran its course and it was time for me to move on. Life with Misha was a part of my past, besides Lauren did a damn good job of helping me forget all about her. After she left I sat down to watch a game of basketball. Sports was always a good distraction. I would be heading over to club Seduction around ten o'clock. Lauren said she wanted me there to celebrate. They finished production on her new commercial so she wanted to pop bottles after the showing of the commercial on a projection screen. I couldn't be happier for her if I tried. I was going to try my best to forget about seeing Misha today and focus all of my attention on Lauren.

I dozed off during the game and woke up to the sound of a whistle blowing. I sat up to find that I slept for two and half hours. It was nine o'clock. I turned the TV off before jumping up to take a quick shower. I would need to hurry up if I planned on getting there in time to meet Lauren. I was excited to see her, for the first time in a long time I felt good that I didn't have to sneak out of the damn house to see a woman who appreciated all of me.

The warm water felt good against my body. It felt so good I didn't want to get out. After about ten minutes I stepped out of the shower, walked naked to my bedroom and started taking an undershirt and boxers out of the dresser to put on. Tonight was special so I wanted to look extra good. I threw on a pair of indigo straight leg jeans, a navy blue Second Sunday t-shirt, and my black leather motorcycle jacket. On my way to the car, I stopped to double check the house was locked and headed out. In the car I dialed Lauren.

"Hey, pretty lady." I complimented when she picked up.

"Hello, you." She responded playfully.

"I'm on my way over to the club," I told her while backing up the car into the street.

"Ok, I'll have Chris meet you around back. I should be there in about twenty minutes myself." I loved how she pulled strings.

"Ok, sexy lady, see you soon." I waited for her to respond before hanging up. I felt good despite all of the tragedy of the last few weeks. Tonight I was going to party like a free man, I knew that for damn sure. Because what time didn't heal, partying would.

One Great Idea
Misha

Seeing my things packed and waiting for me in the living room hit me like a ton of bricks. Tori really wanted a divorce, we were over. I wasn't signing the papers, I didn't want to end my marriage. Sitting in the cab on my way back to my mother's I thought about my life. I would need to start over, get a job and find my own place. It felt so overwhelming that it made me cry again. I could see how much I didn't appreciate him and now I would have to pay for my actions.

The cab driver stopped at my mom's house and helped me unload all of my things onto the porch. I used my key and started moving everything up the stairs into my old room. I was happy no one was home to see me do my walk of shame. An hour after I came back, my brother Jerry came home. He walked into the kitchen, dropping a flyer in front of me on the table.

"What's this?" I asked before reading it.

"Your girl Lauren doing something at Seduction." He answered. I read over the flyer and it said she was premiering her club's commercials tonight. It was starting at ten. I tossed the flyer to the side.

"I don't feel like going out," I told him. I haven't spoken to Lauren in over two weeks. I didn't feel up for talking, or going out because my husband didn't want me anymore.

"Well, think about it because she's giving out free alcohol. I'll be your date if you want." Jerry tried to comfort me but it wasn't helping.

"I'll think about it." I lied.

I went back upstairs to my new/old room and laid on my bed. I wanted to brainstorm on ways to win Tori back and then a brilliant idea come to me. I jumped off the bed and searched my dresser for a piece of paper and a pen. I found an old black and white notebook. I started working on a letter. My plan could help turn things around, I just hoped it would work. It took me an hour to collect my thoughts well enough for it to make sense. I was so excited I bolted down the steps and found my brother watching TV in the living room.

"I've changed my mind. Let's go to Club Seduction tonight." He looked at me with confusion written across his face.

"Cool, what changed your mind?" he asked curiously.

"I don't know but something tells me things might change real soon." I ran back upstairs quickly. I haven't been out in over three weeks, so tonight it was time to let my hair down, get my groove back and pick myself up from way down at the bottom. My man might be mad at me right now but I am going to put my family back together one piece at a time. I slipped into Tori's favorite black dress, the one he bought me for my birthday. Tonight I would party to my marriage. When me and Jerry got into his old blue Camry I told him to stop at the nearest ATM machine first.

A few blocks down, Jerry pulled up to an ATM with no one else around. I stepped out of the car with my debit card ready in hand. I inserted the card into the machine and punched in the pin number. A message crossed the screen, CARD DECLINED. I reentered the pin number and waited but the same message appeared on the screen. I pressed the button to have the card returned but the machine ate it. I couldn't believe this shit. Tori had my card canceled. This couldn't get any worse. I walked back to the car embarrassed.

"Tori canceled my card," I said to Jerry.

"It's ok Mish, I got you tonight." He tried to comfort me but my temporary bout of happiness was replaced with humiliation and anger.

Three's A Crowd but Four is a party

Lauren

I was giving Misha her space. We've both fell back periodically throughout our relationship so this was normal. I knew she wouldn't feel like coming out to help me celebrate so I didn't invite her, that and I knew Tori was coming. We've been getting closer over the last couple of weeks and it was nice. Arnold, on the other hand, was getting more and more agitated with my lack of attention. He said he couldn't make it to the club tonight because he needed to attend a party his wife was hosting. That was fine by me.

I just hung up with Tori, we were both making our way over to the club. We would probably make it there at the same time. I looked hot in my white one shoulder chiffon cocktail dress. I wanted to look extra special for Tori tonight. The commercials we filmed were excellent, so I planned a few specials for the night. Ladies are free as usual, but everyone who shows up tonight gets two free drinks.

I pulled up to the back of the club and Chris was waiting for me. A few seconds later Tori pulled up. A big smile spread across my face when I saw him step out of his Dodge Challenger. Tonight was going to be me and him. We walked hand and hand into my office. Chris followed behind.

"I'm going to help Mack by the door." Chris excused himself before walking out of the office. He closed the door behind him and immediately Tori pulled me in for a kiss.

"You look good woman." He said between kisses.

"Oh, really Mr. Carter? Well, you clean up pretty good yourself." I kissed him on the neck.

"So, what time are you planning on showing the commercials?" He asked seriously.

"In a few minutes. I'm going to walk around and check on the bartenders first. I want to make sure everyone is doing their J.O.B" I answered. We kissed one more time before I walked over to the office door and walked out. Tori followed but said he was going to head over to the bar for a drink. The music vibrated through the walls with women in short skirts and dresses and men standing around checking out the women in short skirts.

After doing my rounds I headed to one of the downstairs bars to look for Tori. I couldn't see him at first so I decided to get started with my commercial premier. Chris cued the lights and the DJ stopped the music. I took center stage holding the mic I had sitting under the bar counter.

"Hello everyone, I am Lauren Michaels the owner of Club Seduction and I want to thank everyone for coming out. I hope you're all enjoying yourself." I started my speech and the crowd took a moment to cheer.

"Tonight is special and I'm happy you're here to share it with me." I turned to see the projection screen reeling down from the ceiling.

"Here is the premier of Club Seduction's new commercials." I introduced the start of my brand new commercials to the club goers feeling on top of the world. Right, when I was about to step down from the platform I spotted Misha and her brother Jerry standing in the audience. My heart stopped. I couldn't believe she actually showed up. I tried not to panic but if Tori didn't see her, he might approach me with a hug or worse a kiss. She waved at me with a smile on her face.

"Hey." I gave her a hug when I approached.

"Congratulations" Misha whispered into my ear.

"Hey, Lauren." Jerry waved at me.

"Hey Jerry, what's up?" I asked though I really didn't care.

"I saw Tori around here somewhere." I looked around, sweat threatening to damage my dress.

"What?" Misha looked panicked.

"Yeah, he came by to see the commercial premier. I passed out a lot of flyers to drum up interest for tonight." I leaned in so I wouldn't scream over the sound of the projector. Misha's panic turned to anger as she started looking around for Tori.

"Are you ok?" I asked to gauge her anger.

"Yeah, I'm fine but the bastard canceled my debit card. Then he wants to hang out like it's nothing to it. I don't fucking think so." She answered with pure anger in her voice.

"Hold up Mish, please don't start no shit in my club tonight." I didn't feel like acting ratchet but if she took me there I would be more than happy to follow.

"I'm cool, I'm alright." She pretended to calm down but I could still see her temples throbbing. I spotted Tori walking over to me. He had a smile on his face, which meant he didn't see Misha or her brother yet. I tried to warn him with my eyes but he kept coming. A few seconds later he stopped in his tracks, his face went from happy to pissed off instantly. Clapping from the crowd distracted me momentarily. I looked at the projectors and they were done playing my commercials. I couldn't believe this heffa made me miss my commercials with her nonsense. Tori approached with a try to fuck with me face.

"Why you here?" he asked Misha. The DJ started mixing beats again drowning out his question.

"Cause I want to be. Why the fuck are you here?" Misha asked him venom behind her words.

"Lauren, I don't want to disrespect your club so I'm going to go ok?" He looked me in the eye before turning to leave.

"You better leave with your punk ass," Jerry commented and I knew it was only a matter of time before the shit hit the fan. I asked Dom to pass me his walkie talkie so I could radio Chris to have him come over.

"What you say to me?" Tori asked with indignation.

"Hold on, hold on. Please don't start no shit in my club cause I don't have time for it." I stood between the two angry men. Jerry backed down first.

"It's all good, I'll see your ass later." He turned to walk away. I was relieved. This was not how I pictured my night going.

"Look maybe you two should go outside to talk," I recommended to both Misha and Tori. There were things I wouldn't be able to control.

"You know what? I didn't come here to fight so I'm going to go party ok." Misha stated before turning to leave in the direction her brother went in. I was left standing there with Tori. We both looked disappointed. He leaned in.

"Do you want me to leave?" He asked.

"You don't have to, I'm ok knowing you're in the same room as me." I tried to remain cheerful even though it would be hard to boo love with Misha close by.

"To be honest I'm not really feeling the whole being here with her thing." He confessed. I gave him a sexy stare before saying.

"Please, for me. I'll make it worth it later on tonight." He smiled involuntarily and nodded ok. I told him to go mingle, enjoy some of the eye candy but not to touch anything. He laughed but listened. I no longer searched for Misha in the crowd, I wasn't going to let her ruin my night. I felt a hand on my waist, which caused me to spin around. Arnold stood behind me with a big smile on his face.

"Surprise." He shouted over the music. My heart sank, could tonight really get any worse than this?

"Hey," I said unenthusiastically.

"Are you happy to see me?" He asked still looking like a Cheshire cat.

"I am, it's just that I thought you said you weren't going to be here tonight." I covered for my lack of real happiness.

"I wasn't going to come but I told my wife I had a client who needed my help. I just wanted to stop in to see how the premier went." He leaned in to talk to me.

"You just missed the commercials," I said in his ear. I wanted to add that I missed them too but I kept quiet.

"I'm sorry babe, I wasn't expecting you to show them this early. Maybe later we can have our own private viewing." He rubbed my hip. After spending so much time with Tori I wasn't feeling that attracted to Arnold lately. I didn't want him touching me and it was harder to pretend to like him.

"That would be great." I scanned the crowd with my eyes, I spotted Tori drinking a corona close to one of the walls.

"I don't want to get you in any trouble. I'm sure your wife will be upset with you." I began talking him out of staying.

"You're right, I just had to see your sexy ass. Walk me outside real quick." He took me by the elbow, leading me out of the club. The fresh night air instantly cooled my sweating skin. I took a deep breath before facing him.

"I don't like not being able to spend time with my princess." He started.

"I know big sexy but you know I've been busy working on the investment you got me. I've been a bit busy but now that things are taking off I'll have more time to spend with you." I made a false promise.

Arnold was a few days away from being old news but I would play my part until then. I gave him a soft kiss on the lips and stroked his face quickly.

"Now, go home to your wife before she starts looking for you. I'm always here sexy and I'm not planning on going anywhere." I lied. He smiled, leaned in to kiss me again and walked away in the direction of his parked car. I stepped back into the club with its insanely loud dance music, into the sea of beautiful brown faces gyrating, twerking and grooving in time to the music. I searched the club until I spotted Tori.

"Have you seen Misha?" I asked.

"No, I wasn't looking for her ass either." He answered sarcastically.

"Ok, follow me." I pulled him by his hand into my office and locked the door.

"I can't believe she came here tonight." I began a rant while unzipping his jeans.

"What you doing?" He asked seductively.

"I'm taking what's mine." I reached down his pants and grabbed his now throbbing dick in my hands. I wasn't letting Misha, Jerry or Arnold ruin my night. I planned on giving it to Tori in the club tonight and that's what I was going to do. I forced him to lie back on my desk and I yanked my dress up over my ass, pushed my thongs to the side and sat on his hardness.

Tori's guttural moans filled the office, knowing I was pleasing him with hundreds of people on the other side of the door turned me on. I bounced up and down on his dick with one hand on his chest holding me up. His hands were holding my waist.

"Damn girl, why you so damn sexy?" he asked. I leaned down to kiss him. My lips met his pulling me into his world. I drowned out the music, the loud talking behind the door and concentrated on how I was feeling. His hard dick stretched my weak spot. I wanted to ride him forever but a hard knock on my door distracted me. Misha's voice came through the door.

"Lauren are you in there? I need you for a second." I couldn't believe this bitch. She was always needing something. I pretended not to hear her and kept riding Tori into the night. Her knocks became more forceful. Tori helped me get down from his lap and quickly zipped his jeans. He kissed me on the lips before opening the back door where both our cars were parked.

"I'll call you tonight." I nodded before fixing my dress and walking over to the door. I unlocked the latch and swung the door open.

"Girl, I can't do this." She yelled.

"Can't do what?" I asked with a bit of panic in my voice.

"I can't be in the same place with him right now." I couldn't believe this bitch was acting all dramatic over this.

"Come in." I pulled her into the office and closed the door.

"Ok, so what do you want to do?" I asked.

"I'm about to have Jerry take me back to my mom's house." Her eyes started tearing up. This shit was starting to get old. Women cracked me the fuck up. How can you act so miserable about being married one minute and when God grants you your wish and make you single you act all torn up about it? I was beginning to lose my patience.

"Ok, well thank you for coming. Call me when you feel up to it ok we can hang out" I gave her a half-hearted hug and opened my office door again. She looked me in the eye before mouthing the words thanks and disappeared in the crowd.

It was around twelve midnight and my head was starting to hurt. I left Chris in charge of the club so I could go home to lay down. I sent Tori a text message saying I was about to leave. When I stepped out of the back door to my office he was standing by my car waiting for me. I couldn't help but smile.

"What are you doing here?" I asked.

"What? you thought I was going to give you some and run out on you. I was waiting in my car for you." He confessed.

"Are you crazy? You've been waiting out here for an hour?" I asked shocked but pleasantly surprised.

"I can leave if you want me to." He pretended to walk away.

"No" I laughed at his silliness. Tori made me feel special and not just like I was a piece of arm candy he wanted to flaunt around all of his friends. He came back to me.

"Do you want to follow me back to my house?" I asked.

"Sure do pretty lady." He reached for his keys in his pocket. I jumped in my car and headed out slowly. A few seconds later his lights came on and he drove up behind me. *What a night?* I thought to myself. Not only did Arnold make a surprise appearance but Misha decides to show her face after weeks of not talking. It didn't matter now, I was about to take my man back to my house and love up on him before cuddling to a movie.

My club is thriving, it's at the height of the game right now, maybe it was time for me cool things off with Arnold. Tori might be my soul mate and now I had time, money and opportunity to see where things could go.

No Legs to Stand On
Tori

I only felt irritation when I saw Misha and if Lauren

didn't say anything I would have really fucked Misha's

brother up in her club. She thought her brothers were tough

but I already saw Jerry get his ass kicked a few times and

never told her. A big part of me didn't want to leave

Lauren's office when Misha came knocking on the door but

I didn't want to make a scene at her place of business. I

knew she was shadowing my moves at the club, I could feel

her eyes burning a hole in my face. However, I ignored the

hell out of her and continued enjoying my night. Fuck

Misha and her whole trifling ass family. I only cared about

her mom cause she was good to me in spite of how

ridiculous her daughter was.

I followed behind Lauren even though I already knew

the way to her house. I hit play on my dashboard and the

mixed tape she made me filled the car. Something caught

my eye in the rearview mirror making me concentrate on the car behind me. I really couldn't see the model or color because of the dark sky, just the silhouette of a woman. At the corner, Lauren turned left so I followed but so did the car behind me. I told myself to stop tripping.

The streets were pretty much empty only a few stray cars driving by every now and then. I dialed Lauren on my cell and waited for her to answer.

"Hey, babe." She picked up on the second ring.

"I have a crazy feeling we're being followed." I tried not to sound paranoid though I'm sure Lauren would think I was.

"What?" she asked confused.

"It's a car behind me and I think they've been trailing us since we pulled off. Make a right at the next light." She waited until the light turned green before turning right, I crept to the corner and decided not to put my turn signal on instead I banged a right quickly leaving the driver behind me little time to follow. The car behind me drove straight a few feet before hitting reverse and turning right. My heart sped up, they were following us.

"I told you. They just drove straight then hit reverse to turn the corner."

"Speed up," I told Lauren to drive faster on the deserted streets. She did as I told her, leaving me enough room to go faster. The car behind me sped up too.

"I'm about to hang up but I want you to park one block up and wait for me to call you." I was going to park my car and see what happened.

"Tori, what are you going to do?" I could tell she was scared but I wasn't going to lead somebody back to her house.

"Just do it, baby, we'll be cool I'm only going to park the car but I need you to park one block ahead of me ok?" I spoke calmly even though my hands started sweating.

"Ok, be careful." I ended the call, tucked my phone in my pants pocket and looked around for an empty parking spot. The speedometer read forty-five miles per hr. I slowed it down and slid into a parking space abruptly. The car sped by me before I heard skid marks from them hitting the brakes. The sound of their engine hitting reverse and stopping right beside my car. The way the car zigzagged let me know it was Misha's crazy ass, she couldn't reverse for shit.

She jumped out of the car and walked to the driver's side. She had fire in her eyes and both her hands balled into fists.

"Get out your car motherfucka. Get out the fucking car Tori." I knew her ass was crazy but I wasn't trying to catch a case. I hit the unlock button and swung my car door open.

"Why the fuck you following me Misha?"

"Because I can nigga, where the fuck you going huh? You didn't think I was going to find out you canceled the credit cards?" She yelled into the night.

"Take your drunk ass back to your mother's house." I went to reach for my car door but she swung at my back. Her punch stung but not enough to do any damage.

"How the fuck do you think I'm supposed to live Tori?" she kept swinging at me so I turned around and grabbed her arms.

"I don't give a fuck about how you gone live, just like you didn't care about telling me about my son. Take your trifling ass home and sleep on it." I was relieved that she was only talking about money.

"You don't give a fuck? Tori, I'm still your damn wife." She continued her rant.

"No, the fuck you aren't. I'm divorcing your ass so get used to it. Now get the fuck out of my way." I pushed her back and she fell on the ground.

"You hitting me now? You want to fucking hit on me now? Bitch I will fuck your ass up." She stood up and charged me with full force. Misha was unbelievable, I couldn't even see why I wanted to marry her ass in the first place. I knew she was drunk because the alcohol was oozing from her pores. I held her in a bear hug until she calmed down.

"Get the fuck off me. I don't need your ass anyway." I walked her over to her brother's beat up car.

"You better call somebody to come get your drunk ass." I walked back over to my Challenger, revved the engine and reversed out of my parking spot. I looked at her car parked in the middle of the street through my rearview mirror but I didn't care what happened to her anymore.

I spotted Lauren's Jaguar a block away and stopped beside her while rolling my passenger window down. "You ok?" She asked.

"Yeah, I'm cool. Drive home, I'm going to drive a few blocks behind you ok?" I yelled through my window.

"Ok." She nodded her head in agreement. I didn't want to tell her that it was Misha following us. I backed up to let her out of the parking space. Misha's car was still sitting in the middle of the street.

I ignored the guilty feeling that was trying to creep up, telling me it was wrong to leave her like that in the road. She was no longer my responsibility, I was no longer her savior. I no longer felt empathy for anything she had to say, she officially had no legs to stand on in my book. I pulled off without looking back. Lauren turned left and I went right. I would take the long way to her house.

Not so Fast
Misha

When we left the club my brother drove us back to my mom's house. I begged him to let me borrow his car. He was trying to give me grief but I promised I would bring it back in one piece. After I saw Tori in the club, looking like he was actually happy it pissed me off because I am so miserable without him. How could he move on that easy? My irritation grew when I saw him and Lauren talking after I walked away. I tried to tell myself it was nothing but the way he smiled at her pricked my nerves. I drove back to the club but couldn't see his car, I drove around for a few minutes before spotting his Challenger a few cars ahead of me. I decided to follow his ass, not really having a plan if he saw me.

I really didn't mean to charge at him but I'm frustrated as hell. He won't even let me talk to him long enough to explain my side. When he gripped me up and put me back in the car I was pissed off. He was going to hear what I had to say if I had to pin his ass down to say it. I let him think I was done following him for now. I needed a plan but first I was going to drive over to Lauren's house to get her to help me.

I sat there for a few extra minutes to gather my thoughts. I inhaled and exhaled deeply until I felt fine enough to drive and made my way over to my best friend's house. She always knew what to do whenever I needed her before. It felt like eternity at each red light but eventually I rounded the corner to Lauren's block. Before I could pull up to the gate I spotted Tori's silver Challenger driving through it. My heartbeat pumped rapidly. It felt like my lungs were on fire. Why was he going over to Lauren's house? I parked on the street, trying to control my heart rate. I knew I wouldn't be able to drive through the gate without tipping them off.

"Fuck it." I said to myself I would climb the bitch if I had to. I looked around and no one was outside it was almost one in the morning. I took my heels off and walked barefoot on the sidewalk. When I approached the gate I saw how tall it actually was.

"Shit" I cursed to myself. It almost looked impossible to climb until I spotted a gap in between the gate and the concrete wall. I hoisted my dress up so I could climb the small stoop, took another quick look around before pressing my back against the wall. I held my breath and turned my head so I could fit. It took me a few minutes but eventually I was able to slide through. I hopped down onto the ground and jogged over to her house. I was careful where I stepped. The Challenger was parked in front of her door so I knew it was his ass. I walked up to the window and tried to see if I could see anything. She had curtains blocking my view. I couldn't see through at first until I spotted a small opening near the bottom. I stooped to my knees and peered through the bottom of the window.

Her dining room light was on, which gave me just enough light to see Tori standing up in the living room. He was facing the dining room so I couldn't see if he was talking to someone. It wasn't long though before I saw Lauren walking over to the couch wearing a matching panty and bra set. My heart nearly stopped in my chest. I couldn't believe my eyes. Tori put his arms around her waist and they started to kiss. My eyes filled with tears, I couldn't believe her. I expected Tori to do this to me because he was angry but Lauren? We were almost like sisters. I wiped away my tears and talked myself out of kicking the door in.

I watched the two of them strip down to nothing, they fucked on the couch, on the table and went into her bedroom for more. I had something for they ass though. I searched around for a brick I was going to bust the windows out of his car. When I couldn't find anything I did a bold move and walked up to her door and tested the knob. It gave so I pushed it open. I paused for a second to see if an alarm would sound. When nothing happened I tiptoed over to the couch and sat down in the same spot I saw the two traitors fuck in. I was going to wait for them to come back out of the room so I could confront the both of them. I listened to their moans and groans for what felt like forever before I couldn't take it anymore. I felt like I was capable of doing anything. I wanted to kill them both. He was mad at me for placing our child up for adoption when all along his ass had no conscience about fucking my best friend.

Lauren screamed one too many times for my taste provoking me up from the couch. I walked into her kitchen and grabbed a knife out of the drawer. Somebody was going to give me answers. I walked through her hallway, stopping just shy of her bedroom door. It was partially open. Lauren was sitting on top of Tori, with his hands around her waist. I hoped it was good because I planned on making sure they died that way.

With one forceful kick, my foot hit the door slamming it against the wall. They both jumped in surprise. Tori saw me first and threw Lauren from off of him. Lauren screamed when she saw me. I hoped she swallowed her tongue.

"What the fuck?" Tori asked. "How did you get in here?" he continued with his questions.

Lauren grabbed for a sheet to cover herself.

"No, don't cover yourself now bitch. You were having a damn good time on my husband's dick." I screamed at her. Tears began to stream down her face. It made me angrier.

"Misha calm the fuck down." Tori tried to stand up from the bed.

"Sit the fuck down." I waved the knife in his direction.

"Ok, alright." He complied while sitting back on the bed.

"What I did Tori was pretty damn messed up but you know what? I didn't do it out of spite. I was young and I loved your ass so much but I knew you were trying to make something of yourself." I waved the knife around as I talked.

"Call it selfish, but I was thinking about you and your future when I made the hardest damn decision of my life. All I wanted was to give you a chance to live your dreams developing software and shit." I continued. He looked at me gripped with fear.

"Misha, listen." He tried to interrupt me but I wasn't trying to hear shit he had to say.

"I'm not listening to shit, you're going to sit there and shut the fuck up until I'm finished." I yelled at him. Lauren looked like she was trying to reach for something near the bed.

"Bitch, try me if you want to and I swear I will kill your ass tonight." Her hand stopped moving and she looked at me wide-eyed.

"I was wrong for not telling you what I did but I wanted to so many times. I wanted to tell you after the first miscarriage but I couldn't find the words to say. I wanted to tell you Tori. I felt so guilty that I went and found Julie the fucking adoption counselor so I could write him letters. I planned on telling you so we could heal and get passed it but still reach out to him." I started crying. The pain in my chest grew in intensity.

"But I come here and find your ass fucking this bitch, so now I don't give a damn about you being mad at me anymore. Tonight we will be even." I nodded my head up and down. I'm sure I looked like a mad woman but I didn't care. I felt crazy, like I was on the brink of insanity and I would come back to reality after I hurt the both of them.

"Lauren? Why the fuck you want to hurt me like this?" I turned my attention to her.

"Misha, stop acting like your ass don't know. You treated Tori like shit ok? It wasn't like I set out to hurt you." Fear was replaced with boldness as she spoke.

"What I did with my husband wasn't for you to fix bitch." I lunged at her with the knife but Tori caught me.

"Get off of me now before I stab your ass." I yelled at him. He was close enough for me to stab him in the neck or shoulder.

"Ok, ok, calm the fuck down." He tried to calm me but I was beyond that now.

I stepped back enough to be out of reach.

"How long were you fucking her?" I asked never taking my eyes off of his. He put his head down which told me it was for a while.

"How long Tori?" I screamed for an answer.

"Misha, it doesn't matter." His answer said it all.

"Were you fucking this bitch before or after you knew about the adoption?" His answer would determine my level of anger so I hoped he answered it carefully. He didn't answer just put his head down. I watched how Lauren looked at the back of his head.

"You want to answer that? Huh? You backstabbing, can't get your own man, piece of shit ass bitch?" My eyes were now fixed on her face.

"Misha put the knife down. We can all be adults and talk without you waving a knife at people." She tried to reason with me.

"Did you just say be adults? Bitch what's so grown up about fucking someone else's husband?" I asked

"I hope you wore a condom because her trifling ass fucks both you and Arnold on the same damn day. Yeah, bitch I saw you walk out of the club with Arnold tonight." Tori's temple twitched which meant that made him mad.

"Oh, what you thought she would stop fucking his ass for you? Wake the fuck up Tori, I was a lot of shit in our marriage but I never stepped out on you. You choose to fuck the bitch who fucks every married man in Atlanta for money oh excuse me for clubs." Lauren jumped up from the bed like she might try to hit me.

"If you didn't have that knife bitch I would beat the shit out you." She yelled at me, sitting on her knees completely naked.

"I'll set the knife down bitch so I can see you try." I was seriously ready to fuck her ass up. Tori stood up from the bed.

"Misha calm down, let's talk outside of the room." He stood up again. I knew he was trying to give Lauren an opportunity to call the police or someone else to come save their dumb asses.

"I don't want to talk to you anymore. You said your piece, you want a divorce and you'll get one no worries, but I'm taking it all bitch. I'm taking every fucking thing you have. Lauren, you can kiss your motherfucking club goodbye." I threatened her, making her eyes grow big.

When Shit hits the Fan
Lauren

I was just getting into my groove when I heard the door slam against the wall. Within moments, Tori was tossing me aside and then I saw her. I couldn't believe Misha was in my bedroom. A loud scream escaped my throat because I was scared as shit seeing her with a knife. I sat listening to her rant but I kept thinking about reaching for my cell phone. She spotted me so I let it go. I wasn't planning for this type of drama Tori wasn't acting like he planned on stopping her crazy ass either.

The minute she started talking about Arnold I knew I would fuck her up when the time permitted. Tori looked mad when she said I was still fucking Arnold like his ass really thought I would stop seeing my sugar daddy.

"Misha, let's just go talk in the other room." He tried again to get her to move out of the room.

"Hell no. Yall like the bedroom and the fucking couch and the table. This is how things are going to go down." She kept waving the knife in the air like a mad woman. I knew she was mad but I needed to get out of this shit alive.

"Misha, listen I'm sorry. I never meant to hurt you ok? Shit just happened." I started the conversation.

"She's right, look we can talk about this Mish." Tori chimed in. Her face didn't soften but got more enraged.

"Then answer my fucking question. How long were you two fucking?" I knew if he told her the truth she would snap and we both would end up on the front of tomorrow's newspaper.

"A few months ago," Tori spoke

"Recently." I blurted out at the same time. Why the fuck would he be honest at a time like this.

"Months ago? Fucking months ago?" Her voice elevated. I grabbed my alarm clock resting on the nightstand and hailed it at her. It hit her against the shoulder knocking her back for a second. That was all I needed, I jumped off the bed and went to grab for the knife. She sliced my face, then my forearm. Blood began squirting from the open gashes. Tori knocked me off of her and took her by the hand holding the knife. She still swung at my face with her free hand but missed.

"Lauren sit the fuck down." He yelled at me. I couldn't believe he would yell at me for trying to get us out of this situation.

He grabbed the knife from her hands and tossed it across the room by my closet floor. My eyes followed it in case I needed to use it.

"Get off of me Tori." She looked like a rabid dog, foaming at her mouth.

"Misha calm the fuck down." His tall, naked muscular body was holding Misha from behind. She thrashed around trying to get free.

"No, get your hypocritical ass hands off of me bitch. I hate your ass and I swear you're gonna pay for this shit." She screamed.

I was tired of the bullshit so I walked over to her.

"Misha get the fuck over yourself, you didn't deserve his ass and you still don't. You're a weak bitch who don't know how to treat a man and that's why his ass came over to me. I treat him way better than your ass ever have. Let her go Tori so I can fuck her up. She ain't that big without the knife in her hands".

She wasn't going to come up in my house being disrespectful and think I was going to sit back and tolerate her bullshit. I let her speak her piece because she had a weapon but I knew I could take her ass. Blood flowed from my face onto my collarbone and chest. I wasn't thinking about that at this very moment but I would beat the shit out of her for marking my face.

Tori turned to look at me and rolled his eyes in my direction.

"Lauren, please take a seat. I don't need you fanning the fucking flames by talking shit." He snapped. I couldn't believe him right now. He looked down at Misha still in his arms.

"Can I talk to you out there?" he asked with a calm voice.

"For what?" she yelled at him.

"I'm asking nicely, next I'm going to pick your ass up and take you in there." He answered.

"Give me her fucking cell phone. I'm not leaving the room without her fucking phone." She yelled in his face.

"She's not getting my fucking phone." I snapped at him. They both were crazy if he thought I was going to give her my phone.

"Lauren give her the phone." He looked me in the eye and commanded that I hand over my phone. I shook my head no.

"Just give her the damn phone." The base in his voice was threatening. I walked over to the nightstand grabbed my phone and threw it at her. It dropped just shy of her chest, falling with a thud on the floor. Tori bent them both over and picked it up. When he readjusted himself he lifted Misha over his shoulder and carried her out of the room like a buff ass caveman.

Mixed Emotions
Tori

I walked Misha out of Lauren's room over my shoulder. She didn't give me much fight but I knew she wasn't done acting out. I thought I would have a heart attack when I saw her standing in the doorway. I knew she didn't want to kill us because she would have come in swinging without giving us a chance to prevent it.

I sat her on the couch and stood over her for a second before I remembered I was naked. I reached for my boxers on the floor by the couch and slipped them on.

"I know this looks bad." I wanted to reason with her. I couldn't believe how guilty having her see me with Lauren would make me feel. I forgot about being mad at her.

"No shit, but you know what I hope it was worth it. I'm done with you and our marriage, ain't those the words you used?" she started to laugh with tears running down her face. I really didn't have anything to say. A few hours ago I was sure about ending my marriage but now I felt torn. I knew I pushed her to this extreme because Misha hated not being heard. I still didn't know how she got through the gates.

"Tori, I only wanted you to let me explain. If you wanted to walk away after that I would have dealt but nooo not you. You couldn't wait to end things so you could continue fucking my best friend. So go ahead and have her, I hope she willing to take care of your ass cause when I'm done I'm getting it all." She threatened. I knew she wasn't lying either. I was about to be taken for a ride. For as long as I was mad at her I knew she wouldn't ask for anything but the tides suddenly turned in her favor. I was fucked and hated that I didn't force her to sign the papers before she found me like this.

It took me thirty minutes to talk Misha into leaving with me. Lauren was still pissed and started talking more shit making it more difficult to leave. I grabbed my clothes and grabbed Misha, making sure she left Lauren's phone on the coffee table. I put her in the Challenger and forced Lauren to buzz us through the gate.

"Where's your brother's car?" I asked looking around for it. She didn't answer just stared out of the window. I finally spotted it a block away from Lauren's house. I would have to come back for it.

I drove us back to my house. I don't know why but I thought it was important for me to keep my eye on her overnight. I didn't need her ass trying to go back to Lauren's house to kill her. I carried Misha into the house and sat her on the couch. She sat like a mummy, lifeless and dazed. I sent Lauren a text telling her I would call her in the morning. She never answered but I couldn't worry about that right now.

Looking at Misha sitting on the couch made me realize I still loved her. When she was telling me why she gave up the baby I remembered how many times I told her my dreams of landing a good job so I could get my mom out of the hood. I told her how my dad walked out, but she knew it was because he couldn't get work and the burden became too heavy. I realized that she wasn't trying to be selfish at all. She sacrificed our son so I could finish school and make something of myself. If we would have kept the baby I wouldn't have finished college and would have gotten a minimum wage job somewhere to support our kid.

She didn't move only stared at her hands like she was in shock. I felt like shit but was paralyzed from guilt. I fucked up and just now saw it. I dropped down on the couch beside my wife and stared into my hands.

Pride Comes Before a Fall
Lauren

As soon as Tori left with Misha I searched for my phone and called the police. I couldn't believe he chose to leave with her delusional ass. A policemen buzzed my intercom ten minutes later. I told him what happened with Misha trespassing onto my property and how she cut me. I conveniently left out the part that she caught me in bed with her husband. I showed them the slice across my face and my arm and gave them the knife she used to do it. He took my name and number and wrote a report on the incident. I told him Misha's full name and her mother's address. I couldn't remember Tori's address by heart. When the officer left I went in the bathroom and took a picture of my face and arm in case I needed it later. The gash was only on the surface of my skin. It didn't cut deep enough to leave me permanently scarred or at least I hoped not.

I threw on a pair of black and yellow yoga pants and a yellow tank top shirt to drive myself over to the ER. I wanted it on record that she did this shit to me. Her crazy ass was going to pay for slicing my fucking face. I pulled my hair up in a ponytail and grabbed a box of napkins so I could keep them pressed to my cheek to stop the bleeding. Before I walked out of my condo I sent my dad a text and then I sent a text to Arnold telling them I was on my way to the ER. Arnold responded first asking which hospital. I told him where I was going and walked out to my car. I walked around the entire car to make sure she didn't do anything to my Jaguar before I got inside.

My cell rang, it was my dad.

"You ok?" He asked sounding a bit groggy but concerned.

"Misha sliced my face and my arm with a knife," I told him through clenched teeth.

"What? Are you kidding me? Your best friend Misha?" He asked in disbelief.

"Yes dad, my ex-best friend. I'm on my way to the hospital." I gave him the name of the hospital before he hung up. I knew he would be on his way. I almost felt bad for making him get up this late to go to a hospital for such a small cut. With Tori gone I needed someone to make me feel special. My ego was more bruised from him leaving with her than the cuts Misha left on my body. I wanted the police to handcuff and escort her crazy ass out of my condo and me and him to curl back up like shit ain't ever happen but he felt the need to leave with her ass like I didn't mean shit.

I sped over to the hospital in the darkness of night with virtually no other traffic to slow me down. Arnold was already there as I pulled up. He ran over to my car wearing a pair of sweatpants and a gray t-shirt. I never saw him dressed casually so it was a real surprise. He hugged me as soon as I stepped out of the hospital, then held me back to see my face.

"What happened?" he asked with concern written all over his.

"I got into a fight with my best friend and she grabbed a knife and stabbed me." I lied.

"Did you call the police? We're pressing charges, her ass must be crazy. The same girl I met the day at the restaurant?" he asked to clarify. I only nodding my head yes. We both walked into the ER and I signed in. I was told to take a seat in the waiting area.

"Don't worry about the bill I'll cover it." He spoke into my ear. He had his hand up to my chin when my father walked in. My dad looked passed him and into my face.

"Are you ok?" he asked with concern written all over his face. I saw how he looked over the cut on my arm and cheek. The bleeding slowed up substantially but I still held a tissue up to it. For a brief moment, we all sat in awkward silence. My dad's fiancé Shannon came in a few minutes later. Arnold's body stiffened. I looked at him then back to her. My dad turned to face Shannon.

"Hi." She put her hand up to wave.

"Dad this is Arnold, my boyfriend. Arnold this is my dad and his fiancé Shannon." I introduced everyone but Arnold didn't look like he wanted to speak to her.

"My dad extended a hand and gave Arnold a death stare. I wasn't sure what all was going on but it made me feel uncomfortable.

"Nice to meet you again." My dad said first. Arnold took his hand to shake it but looked uneasy.

"Again?" I asked turning to face Arnold.

"Yes, Arnold is my brother in law." Shannon stared at him hardcore. My heart dropped into my shoes.

I couldn't believe how small the world was. Beads of sweat formed on Arnold's brow line.

"Weren't you just at the dinner her sister was having?" My dad asked incredulously. Arnold's wife was throwing a dinner for Shannon earlier. Now it made sense why he said he couldn't come to the commercial premiere at the club earlier today. I felt embarrassed standing in front of my father claiming to be dealing with a married man, who was also his age. If my dad really knew why I was at the hospital he would have cursed me to my grave.

Shannon turned to leave the hospital and Arnold ran after her. I was certain he was going to make sure she didn't call his wife. My dad looked angry and I couldn't find the heart to look him in his face. He sat beside me, silent for a few minutes.

"Lauren, what are you doing?" I could hear the pain in his voice. I was caught twice in one night. This was definitely not what I had in mind when I called them both here.

Things go up in Smoke

Lauren

I almost couldn't find the heart to tell the nurses what
happened to my face, especially since it was really a partial
truth but I did it anyway. They put it on record that I was
sliced with a knife by an ex-friend during a shouting match.
I was given painkillers and sent on my way. The skin
wasn't cut deep enough to require any stitches. My dad
gave me a long hug and told me to drive home carefully.
He offered to follow behind me to be sure I made it there
safely. I politely declined, deciding to take the drive of
shame alone. I didn't know where Arnold went but if I
could guess it was back at home trying to talk to his wife
before Shannon decided to tell on him.

Without thinking about it, I drove past my exit and
continued on in the direction of the club. I couldn't stand
the idea of going back home to be alone. My foot went

heavy on the gas as I gunned it back to the only place that made me feel important. I parked around back in my usual spot. The club has long since closed. I used my key to unlock the door and stepped into my office. It felt hollow with no one there. I flipped the light switch on and sat at my desk. The weight of the world came tumbling down and I cried alone at my desk.

I couldn't believe that Tori would leave me alone instead of giving Misha's ass the boot. I saw the way he looked at her like he still cared, even after everything I've done for him. I did everything that a good woman should do for her man. Maybe he was only dropping her off I tried to reason with myself cause there was no way he was actually considering working things out with her. I wiped tears away with my fingertips. I stood up from my desk to check around the club. Maybe I just needed to keep my mind busy.

I pushed the disappointed look of my father's face when he saw that Arnold was my boyfriend out of my mind. I hated seeing how hurt he looked being in that position. I was sure he would be up with Shannon for the rest of the night debating on what should be done. The only lights on in the club was those behind the bar. I walked over and reached for a glass to pour myself a drink. I wasn't a mix master but I knew how to mix vodka with cranberry juice and a few cubes of ice. I sat on a stool at the bar and checked my messages. Nothing from no one. I felt beyond empty.

After my second drink, I started smelling the faint scent of smoke. I stood up and walked around the club to see if there was a smoky outlet somewhere. I couldn't find anything but the smell of smoke was becoming more noticeable. I ran upstairs to the second level but there was nothing. I searched behind the booth seats where I knew there were electrical outlets. I couldn't see anything. A moment later I heard my car alarm going off in the back of the building. I ran down the stairs with fear gripping my heart. I couldn't get to my office fast enough, I swung open the door and tried to get to the back door but the heat on the knob prevented me from opening it. The palm of my hand felt on fire. My car alarm whined loudly and I couldn't get through the back door.

A loud boom pierced the air, shaking me through my core and then something crashed against the back door making me fall backward. I ran out of the office, back into the main part of the club. There was a cloud of thick smoke burning at my eyes. I began coughing and covered my nose with my tank top shirt while running for the front door. When I reached it the knob was red hot. I couldn't turn it, fear paralyzed me by the door. I forced myself to move.

"Where is my phone?" I tried to remember where I placed my phone, it was no longer in my pockets. I ran back over to the bar.

My phone was close to dying but I dialed 911 quickly. I was never happier to hear the operator. I coughed into the phone.

"Please send help. My building is on fire. I can't get out." I yelled into the receiver.

"Ok, calm down ma'am, tell me where you are?" she spoke to me calmly.

"I'm at club Seduction, all of the knobs on the door handles are too hot for me to open." I tried to calm down but I started feeling light headed.

"Is there the presence of smoke?" she asked calmly

"Yes, please send someone now. I'm scared I'm trapped and can't get out." I panicked. She was too calm for me at the moment.

"The fire department is on their way right now. Stay on the line with me. Are you able to put a wet rag to your nose?" She directed me to the faucet. I ripped my shirt off and put it under the sink behind the bar. After I wet it I placed it against my face. It helped with the burning sensation. I ducked behind the bar and begin to bargain with God. I really didn't want to die tonight.

Had I been able to see outside I would have seen the image of a brown woman with curly hair walking away from the club with a gas can in her hand. Instead, I only saw my life flashing before me. I could only see the back of a fully stocked bar. I was left alone with my thoughts, my sins, and my regrets. I listened to the operator telling me to remain calm. The air became too thick to breathe in, so I took long and deep pulls of the air through the shirt. I would need to wet it again soon. The operator's voice became faint, my eyes became heavier. I could hear the sound of sirens in the distance right before I passed out.

To Be Continued....

Part 2 coming soon.

About the Author

K.C Blaze is a very active fiction writer. She wrote her first urban fiction tale a few years ago and hasn't looked back since. She owns Urban Fiction News Magazine and has her own radio show Urban Fiction News Radio. Both are dedicated to providing writers with information on every aspect of publishing from beginning to end. She loves creating lively characters that jump out of the page and into the hearts, mind and souls of her reader. For more information on K.C visit any of the links below.

www.urbanfictionnews.com

platinumfiction@yahoo.com

Twitter: @26kessa

05 9060290

CPSIA information can be obtained
at www.ICGtesting.com
Printed in the USA
LVHW04s0023061018
592623LV00006B/98/P